AMERICAN
VAMPIRE

/ / / /

J.R. RAIN

THE VAMPIRE FOR HIRE SERIES

Moon Dance

Vampire Moon

American Vampire

Moon Child

Christmas Moon

Vampire Dawn

Vampire Games

Moon Island

Moon River

Vampire Sun

Moon Dragon

Moon Shadow

Vampire Fire

Midnight Moon

Moon Angel

Vampire Sire

Published by
Crop Circle Books
212 Third Crater, Moon

Printed in the United States of America.

ISBN-13: 978-1545371640
ISBN-10: 1545371644

Dedication

To all of you who dream of change. May you take those first, tentative steps towards creating the life you've always wanted. Follow your heart always, my friends, and may you make this world a better place.

Acknowledgments

A big thank you to Sandy Johnston (again!), Eve Paludan and Elaine Babich, always my first readers. All writers should be so lucky.

"We're all kept alive by magic, Sookie. My magic's just a little different from yours, that's all."
—*True Blood*

"There are real monsters who walk the earth."
—*Diary of the Undead*

Chapter One

The night was cool.

The waning moon hovered just above the old downtown buildings, its silver light suffusing with the yellow of the parking lot lights. Both sets of lights served to illuminate the tall man standing in front of me. Not that I needed much light to see him in the dark, thanks to the phosphorescent streaks of incandescence that seemed visible only to me. And perhaps others like me.

A small wind rattled a tree next to me. The tree had thick, waxy leaves that reflected the surrounding light. The tree didn't seem native to Southern California. Trees in Southern California tended to be stunted and pathetic-looking. A plastic grocery bag scuttled halfheartedly across the parking lot, passing between Fang and me. We both ignored it.

"Aren't you going to say something?" he asked, grinning easily. There was humor in his deep voice, but there was also something else. Doubt. Just a shred of it. But it was there, underlying his humor. And I knew the reason for his doubt, for I shared it, too. Fang wasn't at all certain this meeting was a good idea, either. And I suspected why.

He has a secret, too. A big secret.

How I knew this, I wasn't sure. A psychic hit, perhaps. But I was suddenly certain that Fang stood to lose much by this meeting; after all, his past—whatever it was—would not remain hidden, not with me in the picture.

We all have our secrets.

I finally moved my hands away from my mouth and took in a lot of air. I don't generally need a lot of air; in fact, I'm fairly certain I don't need *any* air at all. But breathing deep helped calm my nerves, and since my lungs still worked, I figured I might as well use them every now and again.

I also found myself scanning the parking lot, wondering if I had somehow walked into an elaborate prank...or something far worse. A trap perhaps. But I sensed no danger here and I sensed no malice from Fang. Granted, my sixth sense wasn't foolproof, but in situations like this, well, it certainly would have been triggered. Especially since my extrasensory perception seemed to be getting stronger and stronger of late.

"Don't look so concerned, Moon Dance," Fang said. He eased himself off the fender of his car and faced me. "We're alone."

I still hadn't spoken. Music pumped from the bar nearby and I might have heard the sharp crack of a pool ball striking another pool ball. Either that, or someone had just broken a kneecap. There was a slight hint of beer on the wind...and vomit. The two often went hand in hand, especially at this late hour and especially in a back alley parking lot.

I stopped scanning the surrounding area and focused on the man before me. Now with my shock abating, the investigator in me was surfacing. The man, I was certain, had stalked me. In fact, I was sure of it. That raised all sorts of alarm bells within me, although I should have known it would happen sooner or later. Fang was, admittedly, a vampire aficionado. I should have known he would have used all the clues I had laid out before him over the years to eventually find me.

Perhaps you wanted to be found, Sam.

Perhaps.

Granted, a part of me had hoped Fang would be Kingsley, but Kingsley was a very different kind of creature of the night. In the end, I knew that Fang could not have been Kingsley.

But I never expected the man standing before me now.

Finally, I spoke. "They let you off work early." Now I, too, stepped away from my van.

"Yeah, well, I told them it was an emergency," said Fang easily.

He moved away from his car and stepped over

the crumbling concrete parking curb with its exposed, rusted re-bars.

"And this is an emergency?" I asked.

His face lit up. "Of the highest order, Moon Dance."

Now he was coming toward me, moving across the empty parking lot. On his chest, the two great shark teeth swung and bounced from the leather strap. Only I was beginning to think they *weren't* shark teeth.

Fang. His name is Fang for a reason.

More deep breaths. I was tempted to step away from my van, but I couldn't make my legs work. In fact, they suddenly felt gelatinous and heavy and not really my own.

I put my hand on the van's warm hood, stabilizing myself.

Fang was a tall man, and his long strides quickly ate up the asphalt between us. When he was just a few arms lengths away, he stopped, chest heaving.

"I don't know your name," I said, suddenly self-conscious. His eyes rapidly roamed over me, taking me in. But I was used to him looking at me, wasn't I? After all, I had often caught him looking at me.

"You never asked for my name," he said.

"Married women don't ask bartenders for their names," I said.

"You're not married now."

"Technically I'm separated. The divorce

paperwork is being drawn up now by my attorney."

"You're doing an awful lot of talking," said the Heroes' bartender, smiling at me again. His white teeth shone brightly, and so did the monstrously long teeth dangling from his neck. "And not enough asking."

"Fine," I said, feeling my heart calming down. This was Fang, after all, my best friend, my confidant, the man I had opened my life up to...all my secrets, all my fears. Everything. "What's your name?"

"You can call me Eli Roberts," he said. "But my given name is," he paused. "Aaron Parker."

I blinked, and might have gasped, too.

Aaron Parker. I knew the name, of course. Anyone in law enforcement would know the name. I looked at the man in front of me again...looked at the fangs hanging from the leather strap. Indeed, those *weren't* shark teeth.

"You're the American Vampire," I said.

He smiled and laughed lightly. "Could you say that a little louder, Moon Dance?"

Chapter Two

The Downtown Bar & Grill was a new restaurant in a very old building. The walls were brick and the black lacquer bar counter was epic. It stretched from nearly end to end and I could only imagine how many drinks had been served from its polished, scarred surface.

Aaron Parker, aka Fang, found us a table in the darkest corner of the deepest part of the lounge. Music thumped from nearby speakers. There wouldn't be a soul on earth who could overhear us. A waitress materialized out of the darkness like a ghost and took our orders. Aaron ordered for us. White wine for me. Jack and Coke for him.

"You remembered what I drink," I said. I found myself feeling wary and highly exposed and vulnerable. I also found myself fighting a very strong desire to run. But to run was to leave a lot of questions unanswered.

To run was to screw everything up, and I didn't want to screw everything up.

Aaron sat forward and studied me intently. I don't like to be studied intently. He knew that, didn't he? Interestingly, his look was the same look he'd given me many times at Heroes, a bar I frequented with my sister. Silly me, I had thought his probing glance had been an interest of a different sort. Now I knew differently. He had been stalking me. He had known who I was all along.

I instinctively looked away, feeling a bit like a freak at a carnival: *"Come one, come all—see the real-life bloodsucker!"*

Now that he was sitting across from me and not endlessly serving customers, I had a chance to really study him. I had always found him attractive. I'm sure he knew that. And my sister had an unhealthy crush on him that her husband really should probably be concerned about. Aaron Parker was tall. Perhaps one of the tallest men I had ever seen. I suspected he was an athlete and I resisted the urge to ask him if he played basketball. Aaron had full lips. The kind most women drool over. He had sad puppy dog eyes, as brown and bright as polished cherry wood. But it was his mouth that I found the most curious. He didn't seem to know what to do with those beautiful lips of his. Sometimes he pulled them as if snarling. And sometimes they seemed to drape over his lower lip. Often they moved and shifted and I kept having the impression he was about to say something, but words rarely followed the movement. It was the oddest twitch I had ever seen.

Finally, his moving lips formed words. When he spoke, he did so softly. If not for my better-than-average hearing, I might have missed what he said: "I remember everything you tell me, Samantha."

"Except I never told you my name."

Now he looked away, suddenly embarrassed. He should be embarrassed. He had stalked the shit out of me. "Yes, I've known your name for some time."

"It's not nice to stalk people," I said. "Especially someone who can kill you and deposit your body somewhere over shark-infested waters where it will never be seen again."

Aaron's eyes flashed briefly with amusement. "It was a chance I had to take."

Our drinks came. It was late Sunday night and the bar crowd was thinning. No doubt only the hardcore drinkers were left...and a creature or two of the night. As we sat in the bar, toasting to good health and long life (which put a smile on my face), I was suddenly certain Aaron and I were being watched. I glanced over his shoulder, searching for the source, but there was only an empty stairway leading up to God knew what. Still, the electrified field that only I seemed to see, a field that consisted of glowing streaks of light that helped me see into the darkest of nights, seemed to be buzzing with more than usual activity. Light streaks zipped about as if energized by something unseen.

Something's coming, I suddenly thought. What that was, I didn't know.

I turned back to Fang. "So how did you find me?" I asked, although I had already intuited the answer. Obviously, I had given the man enough clues about my life—in particular, the cases I had worked on—for him to find me. Quite simply, he had put two and two together. Even if *two and two* had come over the course of years.

He confirmed my hunch, and explained. To his credit, he looked a bit sheepish. Anyway, it had been one of my bigger cases four months ago that had gotten some national attention, a case that involved a runaway girl and a murderous dad. Despite my best efforts to remain anonymous, my name had appeared once or twice in the newspaper. I had, of course, mentioned to Fang that I was working on an important missing person case. By this point, I had already inadvertently dropped enough clues over the years to direct him to the general region where I lived. And once he knew the general region, well, it had just been a matter of scanning the local headlines for any news about a runaway.

I said, "So everything I ever told you...."

"I made notes," he said. "I saved our messages. I pored over them later, searching for hidden clues about you. About how to find you. In the beginning, you gave me very little to work with. But you loosened up over the years."

I wasn't sure how I felt about that. There was a

creep factor here that was hard to ignore. But I also understood human nature. Or, at least, tried my damned best to. Yes, of course he had been curious about me. Who wouldn't have been? I was a woman who was professing to be much more than a woman. And, admittedly, I had certainly been curious to find him, too, but I had never acted on it. I was a married woman at the time, working hard to keep things happy and seemingly normal.

Too hard.

A marriage shouldn't have to be so much work. Love shouldn't crush your soul. A relationship should add to your life, not take away from it. Something I'm only now beginning to understand.

But it was hard to remain mad at Fang...or Aaron. There was a gentleness to him that I never saw coming. His instant messages to me had exuded confidence. But I wasn't seeing the confidence here. No, I was seeing a man, perhaps in his late twenties or early thirties, who had anything but confidence. I was missing something here, and I wasn't sure what it was.

I looked again at the teeth dangling from his neck. They were long and thick—but not quite as thick as shark teeth. They looked like dog canines. Big dog canines. I looked again at his twitching mouth, and saw him curl his upper lip down as if to....

As if to cover two massively prominent canines. Two unnaturally long canines.

"Those teeth," I said, motioning to his chest.

"Are yours."

"Why, Moon Dance," he said, and I sensed his old charm. "You are quite the detective."

Chapter Three

I knew the story of the American Vampire, of course.

In essence, a young man with two extraordinarily long canine teeth had sucked his girlfriend dry. His trial had been as sensational as they get, and who could forget the images of the young man opening his mouth and exposing those two insanely long canines for all the world to see.

And here he was. In the flesh. Sitting across from me. A young man who had been tried and convicted of murder. A young man who had been deemed criminally insane. And there were very few who would argue that point.

And he's Fang, I thought. *This is crazy.*

If I looked hard enough I could see the similarities, but the truth was, he looked nothing like the tormented young man whose image had been broadcast across the airwaves and newsrooms and the early Internet. Now his thick beard would make him nearly impossible to place, and I was almost certain he had had some nose work done. And as I looked again, I could see he was wearing brown contact lenses. Almost certainly his eyes had been blue originally. But the biggest difference was his great height. He had not been quite this tall when he was eighteen years old. Then again, it was hard to know for sure, since he had often sat petulantly next to his attorneys. Still, I would guess he had grown another five inches...perhaps enough to completely throw authorities off his trail.

He was, after all, an escaped convict—and allegedly responsible for two more deaths. A guard at the criminally insane prison and the owner of a creepy museum in Hollywood who had purchased Aaron's teeth for a morally questionable display.

A sick display. There had been an outrage, of course.

But the outrage became moot when the owner had been found dead some months later, and the teeth had been stolen.

The same teeth that now dangled from Fang's neck.

The same fangs.

"You are a killer," I said.

"As are you, Samantha," he said, sitting back and sipping casually on a drink that smelled strong enough to preserve a warthog. "We are both victims of circumstance. Never forget that."

His faux brown eyes continued scanning my

face. I could see the wonder in them; I could sense his awe. His thoughts were alive to me, nearly registering in my mind as my own. After all, I had a deep connection to Fang, deeper than I had ever thought possible with another human being, and although the man in front of me was largely a stranger, now that we've met in the flesh, our connection seemed only to intensify.

He closed his eyes and took in some air. "I can feel you, Moon Dance."

I blinked. "Feel me how?"

"In my head. You're there. In my thoughts. Just off to the side. Listening. Picking up words here and there."

He cocked his head slightly to one side, like a dog listening to something on the wind. Now it was my turn to study his face. The man was gorgeous. Of that, there was no doubt. After all, there was a reason why my sister turned into a gibbering idiot every time he served us a drink. His brown hair was jauntily disheveled, or perhaps messily windblown. Mostly, it was his lips that commanded my attention. So full, especially the lower one. There was a spot of liquid on the bottom one and all I could think of doing was tasting that spot. Just that one, sexy spot.

His eyelids quivered, where I saw a brief flash of white, and realized his eyes had rolled up into his head. "Yes, there you are, Moon Dance."

I said nothing. Music continued pumping through the bar. A very old drunk man got up from his stool and started slow dancing with himself. He spun himself once, twice, and I thought he might even dip himself, but luckily he bumped into the bar and grabbed hold of it. No one seemed to notice him but me.

And seemingly inside my skull, I heard a very faint, yet very distinct whisper: *Hello, Moon Dance.*

Fang opened his eyes and smiled at me.

"Okay," I said. "*That's* never happened before."

Chapter Four

"It is common knowledge that vampires can control others with their minds," said Fang.

"But I'm not trying to control you," I said.

"Yet," he said. "But if I find myself suddenly giving you a pedicure, I might suspect otherwise." He winked.

I lifted my hand. "Trust me, there isn't a file strong enough for these nails."

"Let me see your nails, Moon Dance."

"No."

"Please."

I sighed and held out my hands. He took them gently and did not flinch at the extreme cold of my flesh like most do. Indeed, shivering and smiling, he seemed to revel in the iciness. He next tapped the tip of my index finger. I felt like a horse being sold at auction. "You could disembowel a rhino with these things."

"Or a bartender who lets my secret out."

He grinned again. "I didn't realize how feisty you were, Moon Dance."

"We never had this much at stake, Fang."

"We both hold equally damaging secrets. I, too, am trusting you to keep my secret safe."

"You're a convicted murderer and an escaped prisoner."

"And you're a blood-sucking fiend."

I studied him. The corner of his mouth lifted in a small smile, along with some of his beard. "Fair enough," I said, sitting back. "So what's this mind control business you're talking about?"

He finished his drink and waved the waitress over. I had barely touched my own wine. When she was gone, he sat forward, resting his weight on his sharp elbows. "You have already mentioned your sixth sense, Moon Dance. You have even mentioned that you felt it is getting stronger."

I nodded; it was.

He went on, "Well, your sixth sense is a little more far-reaching than you have thought; at least, that is my understanding."

"How far-reaching?"

"Telepathy. Hypnosis. Mediumship."

"One at a time," I said. "Hypnosis?"

"You've seen *Dracula*, right?"

"Maybe."

"Did you read the book?"

"No."

"A vampire who's never read *Dracula*?"

"I've been busy raising kids and trying to keep a husband happy. At least I'm batting .500."

He smiled sadly. "I'm sorry he hurt you, Moon Dance."

"So am I."

"Want to change the subject?"

I nodded.

"Back to mind control. Dracula, you see, has the ability to induce hypnosis with just his gaze. You might want to look into it."

I shook my head at his silly pun. "Fine. What about mediumship?"

"That's speaking to the dead, either to those who have passed on or still linger."

"Linger?"

"Ghosts, Moon Dance. You should be able to see ghosts."

I scanned our surroundings. The electrified air, usually so alive with light filaments, seemed particularly erratic in here. To my eyes, the streaking lights zigzagged even more crazily, sometimes coalescing into bigger shapes. As I scanned the air around us, Fang continued speaking.

"You are a supernatural being, Moon Dance. A supernatural being in the world of mortals. You should be seeing things I could never, ever imagine."

The squiggly lights in the bar flashed and zigzagged like thousands upon thousands of electrified fireflies. I watched as they whipped crazily around a nearby stairway, a stairway that led up into the black depths. The flashing lights began gathering together, collecting other squiggly lights. I had seen such things before but had dismissed them. They were just strange lights, right? Nothing more.

"Creatures of the night seem to attract each other, Samantha, whether they know it or not...or whether they want it or not. It is not a coincidence that the werewolf came into your life. Soon, I expect others like yourself to make appearances."

"Like myself?"

"Vampires, Moon Dance. You cannot be an island for long. Not in this world of fantastical creatures."

I continued studying the glowing object at the foot of the stairway. More light gathered around it. Now, if I looked hard enough, I could see shoulders, hips, and a head forming. Even what appeared to be longish hair. And then, amazingly, the light creature turned toward me. I couldn't see its features, but I sensed its great pain. And then, buried deep in my mind's eye, I saw a flash of a knife's blade, heard a strangled cry, then weeping, and then...nothing.

"I see a ghost," I said. "There by the stairway."

I saw Aaron turn out of the corner of my eye. "I don't see anything, Moon Dance. But I'm not surprised. This is supposedly one of the most haunted buildings in Fullerton."

And just like that the vaguely humanoid column of light dispersed, scattering into a thousand glowing, fluorescent shards of energy.

Son of a biscuit, I thought, reciting my son's favorite expression.

After a moment, Aaron Parker looked back at me. "So does it feel strange finally meeting me, Moon Dance?"

"Yes and no. A part of me wants to run back to my computer and continue this conversation there. I felt safe there. I felt open. I felt free to be me."

"You don't feel free now?"

"I don't know how I feel, to be honest."

"Do I feel a bit like a stranger?" he asked.

I nodded and I felt the tears come to my eyes. "Yes."

"A stranger who knows your deepest and darkest secrets."

I nodded, suddenly finding it hard to speak.

He said, "Do you regret meeting me, Moon Dance?"

I sat motionless for a long time before I reached out and took his warm hands in mine. As I did so, he curled his long fingers around mine. "I don't know," I whispered, and it was perhaps the hardest three words I have ever spoken.

He continued holding my hands. Now he rubbed his thumb along my knuckles. His thumb was rough, calloused. He was a grease monkey, no doubt. Tending bar at night, fixing up his classic muscle car during the day.

Fang tilted his head slightly. "*Grease monkey* is not a politically correct term, Moon Dance. We prefer to be called lubed primates."

I snorted. "Sounds like a bad porno."

"There are no bad pornos, Moon Dance."

"Eww, and you just read my thoughts."

"Yes," he said. "I heard a few snatches here and there."

"So how is it that *you* can read *my* thoughts?"

"I don't have all the answers, Moon Dance."

"Well, give it your best shot, big guy."

He stared at me long and hard. As he did so, his tongue slid along his lower lip and seemed to be searching for something that was not there. I sensed his great sadness for what was lost. I suspected I knew the source of his sadness.

Finally, he said, "We are connected, Moon Dance. Or, more accurately, you have allowed me access into your mind."

"So I can turn it off?" I asked.

"I don't see why not," he said. "And you're right, Sam, I do miss them every day. More than you know."

His teeth, of course.

Chapter Five

Instead of going home, I went to a place I was familiar with: The Embassy Suites in Brea. My home over the past month.

I parked the minivan in my old spot, and shortly said hello to Justin who was working the front desk. He smiled and nodded and seemed to have forgotten that I had checked out a week earlier. Of course, just last week, when I had busted my husband for running an illegal strip club in Colton, I had dressed the part of a stripper. I might be little, but I'm a curvy thing, and Justin the night clerk hasn't looked at me the same since.

I felt his eyes on me all the way to the bank of elevators. At the ninth floor, I found a locked service door I had seen many times in the past. A service door I had taken note of. Why? Because the plaque on it read: *Roof Access. Maintenance Personnel Only.*

I glanced up and down the hall, took hold of the locked doorknob, and turned steadily until the inner mechanisms shattered in my hand. The knob broke off.

God, I'm a freak.

I pushed the door open, and, after wiping the knob with the hem of my shirt, tossed it in the corner of the stairwell. Next I stepped over a low gate and quickly headed up a metal flight of stairs, taking them two at a time and noticing how strong my legs felt. The door at the top of the landing was locked as well. But not for long.

As pieces of the broken door knob fell away at my feet, I stepped out onto the roof.

Immediately, wind buffeted me. The waning moon was higher now and shone through a thin layer of pathetic-looking stratus clouds. Mostly, though, the sky was clear, and I could even see a star or two.

At the service door, I quickly removed my clothing and naked as the day I was born, moved across the dusty roof, avoiding, of all things, a broken beer bottle.

Hell of a party up here.

Now standing at the roof's edge, I stared down at the city of Brea, which shone before me like a brilliant constellation, providing me a view that the heavens could not. At least, not the heavens here in Southern California. Thousand of lights winked and sparkled. Some were brighter than others—street lamps, perhaps. Others were barely discernible—

bathroom nightlights and perhaps the glows of Kindles and Nooks.

Whatever those were.

The wind was at the edge of the building. It rocked my naked body. But I had no fear of falling. My hair whipped around my head like so many serpents. Medusa would have been proud. Or envious. I breathed slowly, deeply, each intake spiced with exhaust and tar and the sage from the nearby foothills.

The world lay at my feet. The normal world. Where people prayed to God and Jesus, where people worried about their kids' health and Charlie Sheen's career, where life went on steadily and predictably.

Life hadn't gone so predictably for me. Life had hung a hard right turn at "predictable" and detoured through a forbidden forest where the Headless Horseman was real, where werewolves existed, where a mother of two could be changed forever into something nightmarish.

I took in more air and lifted my face toward the heavens. The day's latent heat rose up from the roof's surface, warming my eternally cold buns. I heard honking and tires squealing. The crash of a fender-bender.

Oops.

I heard a baby crying from the hotel below and the steady hum of a hundred or so air conditioners powering through the warm night. The building beneath me seemed alive, vibrating and swaying slightly. Or perhaps that was just my imagination.

I stood there for a heartbeat longer.

And then spread my arms wide and jumped.

Chapter Six

The drop down from this hotel was always a little dicey, although jumping from the roof gave me some extra wiggle room. But not much.

I arched up and out over the roof...and seemed to pause briefly at the apex of the arch. From here I had a glimpse of an ambulance flashing down Birch Street, heading away from me. But there was no sound. No sirens. No honking. Nothing. Time and sound always seemed to subside in these moments.

These wonderful, exhilarating moments.

Now I tilted forward, arms outstretched. A falling, inverted cross.

I picked up speed.

Hair whipping behind me like a failed parachute. Wind thundering over me. The hotel rushing past me.

Someone was standing at the hotel balcony, smoking a cigarette. He never saw me. Or maybe I didn't register in his conscious brain. Maybe tonight he would dream about a curvy, black-haired woman plummeting past his balcony, arms outstretched, and naked as all get out.

I was rapidly running out of floors.

A single flame appeared in my thoughts. The flame burned bright, seemingly in the center of my forehead, no doubt in the region the New Age gurus call the Third Eye. In the center of the flame was a winged creature that would have given anyone nightmares.

Except that winged creature was me.

It was my monster familiar. It was my monster alter-ego. It was one hell of a wicked-cool looking creature.

And it was me.

It waited in the flame, its wings tucked in, elongated head cocked slightly to one side. It always waited for me, ready at my beck and call. My own personal flying demon.

Except *I* was that flying demon.

As the floors swept past me and the concrete sidewalk rapidly approached, I felt myself being pulled to that creature, drawn to it powerfully, supernaturally, miraculously.

The metamorphosis happened in an instant.

The flame disappeared in an explosion of light and when I opened my eyes again, a pair of massive leathery wings—which attached to my wrists and ran down below my knees—snapped taut, slowing my decent. The gravitational force on my wings was incredible, but this new body of mine was more than up to the task. My arms held strong.

I adjusted my arms and angled forward, sweeping nine or ten feet over the ground and just missing a handicap parking sign. It rattled angrily in my wake.

Now I flapped my wings. Yeah, I know. A crazy statement. But these are crazy times.

At least, for me.

I flapped my wings and quickly gained altitude. I found the effort of flying easy. My shoulders were powerful. The thickly membraned wings caught the wind and forced it down and behind me. The sound of my beating wings thundered everywhere at once. Anyone nearby would have heard me. They would have looked up...and seen something they wouldn't soon forget.

My body was aerodynamic and pierced the wind effortlessly.

I continued rising above the glittering city of Brea. Yeah, it was cold up here, but I was perfectly adapted for that, too. Thick skinned. Insulated. Perfectly adapted or perfectly created?

I didn't know which. And I didn't care.

I rose higher and higher. The thrill of weightlessness was so exhilarating that it drove all thought from my mind. Wind whispered over me, seemed to part for me, opened for me new sights few people would ever see or experience.

And still I climbed.

The temperature dropped exponentially. I

plunged into a roiling cumulus cloud and the world briefly disappeared. I was surrounded in ice crystals which was at once serene and mildly disorienting. I shook my great head where the crystals had collected. They broke free and fell away.

The cloud opened and soon I was flying parallel with it, rising and falling with its amorphous contours, like a fighter plane over a desert floor. The movements of my wings were minute, so minute I wasn't consciously aware of making them. The moon shone over my shoulder, reflecting brightly off the cloud's pale surface. My shadow kept pace, rising and falling. A monster's moon shadow. Wings outstretched, flapping almost lazily, I was a massive creature.

The sky above me was clear, filled with millions upon millions of glittering stars. I focused on one such star and flew toward it. What would happen if I just kept on flying? No doubt the deep vacuum of space would wreak havoc on my flying. With no air, I would float aimlessly and endlessly.

I shuddered at the thought.

The cloud dispersed and a great sweeping hillside appeared beneath me, dotted with brightly lit homes. I thought of Fang. The man was a killer, of that there was no doubt. He was also a fugitive. Once, long ago, I had made an oath to uphold the law and bring such fugitives to justice.

But that was then....

...and this was now. Now, I had some dirty secrets of my own, didn't I? Now I had taken one life and was responsible for a second.

Victims of circumstance, Fang had said. I agreed to an extent. Victims were not given a free pass to hurt others.

I flapped my wings languidly, riding along a powerful jet stream, which propelled me forward powerfully, effortlessly. Fang, aka Aaron Parker, aka Eli Roberts (his assumed name) was a beautiful man. There was a reason my sister seriously had the hots for him.

I nearly laughed at the thought that this flying creature could have a sister. And then I almost laughed at the thought that this flying creature could laugh.

Life is weird.

The clouds below opened, and I saw a small plane flying beneath me, buzzing laboriously even as I flew effortlessly and silently. Its lights flashed in accordance with aviation law. There were no laws for giant flying monsters. I was beyond the law. I couldn't give a damn about laws, anyway.

To an extent.

I still had a life to live and children to raise and food to put on the table. By necessity, I had to play by the rules of man.

Yes, Fang was a beautiful man. He was also my closest friend. But everything had changed, hadn't it? He was no longer my anonymous friend who I could open up to about everything. He had a face. A history. A *troubled* history.

He was also, of course, a world-class stalker.

And a killer.

Shit.

Below, I spotted the Hollywood sign, the word so tiny that by all rights I shouldn't have been able to read them. But I could. Giant vampire bats had eagle-like vision.

I dipped a wing and turned to starboard slowly, a great arching turn that took a full minute. The sky was my playground. The clouds my jungle gym.

I completed my turn and innately headed home, following an inner guidance system that was so inherent that I didn't doubt it or question it.

It's good to be me sometimes.

I headed back to the Embassy Suites.

Chapter Seven

I was answering emails on my laptop and watching Judge Judy emasculate this deadbeat dad when my cell phone rang. I picked it up from the coffee table and looked at the faceplate: *Caller Unknown.*

I almost didn't pick up. By nature, I don't like *Caller Unknown* calls. What are people hiding?

The phone rang a second time. And as it did so, an electrical sensation crackled along the length of my spine. As if a ghost had run an ethereal finger down the center of my back.

I shivered. I knew to pay attention to such sensations. Such sensations were strong indications that something important was going on.

The phone rang a third time. Yes, I use old school rings, even for my cell phone. Phones are supposed to *ring*, dammit. Not sing Christina

Aguilera's failed national anthem attempt.

Now Judge Judy was really laying into this asshole again. Reminding him he was the child's father. That he had responsibilities. She also let him know what she thought of him. Trust me, she didn't think very highly. I loved every second of it.

The phone rang a fourth time. My phone will ring five times before it goes to voicemail. The buzzing along my spine continued to crackle. The fine hair on my forearms was also standing on end.

Something's wrong, I thought.

My email was unfinished. Judge Judy continued her verbal berating. I looked at the time on my phone. I had to pick up my kids in a few minutes. Normally, I would have let the call go to my voicemail.

Normally.

"Answer the phone."

The words came from behind me. Except behind me was a wall. I jumped off the couch, screaming and gasping. The voice was soft and whispery and it scared the shit out of me.

I answered the phone, still scanning the room, still scared shitless. Who had spoken to me?

"Hello," I said, feeling my heart beating somewhere near my throat. I was alone in the house. I was sure of it. I would have heard someone enter. I would have *sensed* someone entering.

There was no response from the other end of the line. I headed for the hallway. Scanned it. No one was here. Now from the line I could hear faint breathing. And as I searched the bedrooms and bathroom, I said hello again. And when I got to my own bedroom, a voice finally answered.

And it was the tiniest voice I had ever heard.

"Hi." A girl's voice. Maybe five. Maybe less.

I paused, doing a quick mental rundown of all my nieces and nephews. Although I was not as close to some of my sisters and brothers as I wanted to be, I rarely received a call from any of their children. Still, I could not think of a niece this young.

"Well, hello," I said. "And who is this?" I asked, my own voice rising a friendly octave or two. I glanced in my room. My house was completely empty.

So who had spoken to me?

I didn't know. But I let it go and wrote it off to stress. After all, these past few weeks had not been without their trials. And last night....

Yes, last night.

Last night still had me reeling. Had it really happened? Had I really met Fang?

I had. Oh, yes, I had.

The little voice spoke again over the phone. "I'm Maddie."

"Hi Maddie," I said, switching my focus from the strange voice to the little girl. Just about all the hair on my body was standing on end.

Something's wrong, I thought.

"Where's your mommy, Maddie?" Near my bed, my alarm clock registered exactly 3:00 p.m. I had to leave now to pick up my kids. I had been missing my kids all day; or, rather, ever since I got up a few hours ago. I had an overwhelming need to see them, to hold them, to pull them in close and keep them safe. The feeling seemed particularly poignant and slightly irrational. But now I wondered if something else was going on. I wondered if my sixth sense had picked up on this call long before it had come.

"My mommy got kilt."

Kilt?

My heart stopped. *Killed.* A strong and now not-so-irrational panic had completely replaced any subtle sixth sense I was feeling. A mommy instinct was kicking in, and it was kicking in hard.

"Where are you Maddie?"

"A bad man's house."

"Maddie, baby, where's your dad?"

"I don't have a daddy."

"Who's the bad man, Maddie?"

And now the little girl lowered her voice to a soft whisper and it broke my heart. "He's very very bad," she said. "And he hurted me."

I was standing, pacing. Tears appeared in my eyes. Sweet Jesus. What the hell was going on?

"Maddie, please, honey...where are you?"

"I don't know." More whispering. "It's dark. And cold."

I covered my face. This was real. And my alarm system was ringing off the hook. This was real. This wasn't a prank.

Get information. Get all the information you can.

"Maddie, honey, what's the name of the bad man?"

"He kilt my mom. He shot her. He shot her dead."

"Baby, where are you?"

"I scared."

"Everything's going to be okay, Maddie. Please, honey, do you have any idea where—"

And now the little girl must have pressed her mouth hard into the phone, because her next whispered words were barely discernible. "He's coming!" I heard shuffling, and now I heard her whimpering. "He's coming. I scared. I so scared."

"Maddie—"

And then the line went dead.

Chapter Eight

I stared at my phone, completely rattled. I heard again and again the little girl's tiny voice: *"I scared. I so scared."*

The iPhone soon drifted to sleeper mode, then powered down. I inhaled deeply. There were tears on my cheeks. I relaxed my grip on the phone. Any harder and it would have broken. The call had gone straight to my heart. It would have gone straight to the heart of any mother. Hell, it would have gone straight to the heart of anyone with an ounce of humanity.

I wiped the tears from my eyes and cheeks.

Someone killed her mother. And now someone was keeping her in a dark and cold place. A bad man who was hurting her.

I inhaled. I was rattled, totally shaken. The call had caught me completely off guard. Hell, it would have caught anyone off guard. I found myself, perhaps for the first time in a long, long time, completely unsure of what to do next.

I heard the fear in her voice. I heard again and again her childish attempt to keep her voice quiet.

Who was she? Who was her mother?

And, perhaps the biggest question of all: How had little Maddie gotten my number?

I didn't know. But I was going to find out.

Knowing I was incurring the wrath of my kids' principal, a man who already didn't look very kindly on me, I briefly put off picking them up and called my ex-partner, Chad Helling. One time, not so long ago, I was a federal agent. Now, because of circumstances very much out of my control, I had gone private.

Chad picked up on the fourth ring. I said, "I'm only a four-ring gal now, huh?"

"Be glad I answered on the fourth ring, Sam. I happen to be a very busy federal investigator."

"Uh huh, and whatcha doing now?"

"Waiting in line at Starbucks."

"And it took you four rings to pick up?"

"It took me four rings to hang up on my mom and take your call."

"You hung up on your mom to take my call?"

"Yes. So this better be good."

I told him about the phone conversation with little Maddie, reciting it nearly word for word since it would be forever seared into my memory.

Chad was silent, digesting this. Finally, he said,

"Brave little girl. And savvy."

"Brave and savvy aren't going to be enough," I said. "She's with a monster."

He took in some air, inhaling sharply. "I can look into recent murders. See if anything involves an abducted child, too."

"The mother was murdered recently. There's a good chance she hasn't been found. And may never be found."

"An abduction, then."

"Yes, look for a missing mother and child. There won't be a murder reported. At least not yet."

"And you know this how?"

"Call it a hunch."

"Fine." He paused. "Any chance the child was playing a prank on you?"

"Not a chance in hell."

"Don't hold back, Sam. Tell me what you really think."

"Smart ass."

He said, "My question is: How did Maddie find your number?"

I had been thinking that, too. I bit my lip, and looked at my watch. Shit. I was already seriously late. "Hard to know, but my guess is that the number was already programmed into the phone."

"Her mother's phone? Or the killers?"

"The million-dollar question," I said.

"Maybe Maddie hit redial. Who was your last call?"

I could have smacked my forehead. I told Chad

to hang on as I quickly scrolled through the iPhone.

"A creditor," I said.

"Keep scrolling."

I did. "Nothing unusual. Nothing out of the ordinary."

"Keep looking," said Chad. "Perhaps a past client."

"Nothing," I said. "But I'll go through it again when I'm not in a hurry."

"When you're not in a hurry? Hey, I was the one jonesing for coffee."

"Just please find out what you can," I said. "And tell your mother sorry."

He said he would and before he clicked off I heard him ordering an iced venti vanilla latte...and my mouth watered.

God, I missed coffee.

Still shaken, I quickly scrambled around my house, grabbing my sunhat and my purse. I had already slathered my cheeks and hands with a heavy application of the market's strongest sunblock, although that did little to stop the searing pain as I now dashed out of the house and crossed the small patch of grass that separated my house and the garage. Oh, how I envied those with connecting garages!

I was gasping by the time I reached the minivan. There had to be an easier way to get my kids. Maybe there was, but for now, no one was picking my kids up but me.

When my hot, irritated, inflamed skin had

calmed down, I started the minivan, turned on the AC, and headed out to my kids' school.

Chapter Nine

My kids were being pills.

Anthony had gotten into a fight...with a girl, no less. The girl, apparently, had seriously kicked his ass (and is it wrong that I secretly found this funny?), and as we drove to Burger King, his older sister, Tammy, wouldn't let him forget it. It took the threat of a week's grounding to finally get her to ease up.

I think my boxing trainer, Jacky, might be getting a new client this summer. Someone needed to teach the boy how to fight, and obviously it wasn't going to be his worthless dad. Granted, I wasn't advocating fighting, especially fighting girls, but who wants to hear about their boy getting their ass kicked at school?

"But Mom," said Tammy. "She *sat* on him."

I stifled a giggle behind my hand. Anthony, who was sitting next to me and sporting a swollen lip, looked at me sideways. When I gained some semblance of control over myself, I said, "Then maybe you should protect your little brother and not let girls sit on him."

"Who do you think pulled her off him, Mom?" said Tammy. "I wasn't going to let that cow sit on my brother. Well, not for very long, anyway."

She giggled again, and I did my damndest not to join her.

We pulled up to Burger King and I put in our orders. I repeated Anthony's plain hamburger order twice, knowing he wouldn't touch anything with ketchup or mustard or anything else on it. With our food bagged, we headed home, and while the kids ate and did their homework, I took a hot shower. The shower was intended to clean off the copious amounts of sunscreen, but it also served another purpose.

I craved heat. My body had no natural warmth. I lived with an eternal chill, and so I craved blessed warmth. Showers were certainly nice, but, admittedly, nothing beat the warmth of a man lying next to me, a warmth I rarely felt since my own ex-husband had basically shunned me.

Of course, I had recently experienced such warmth. In fact, just over a week ago, in the arms of another man. A former client of mine. A man with his own dark secrets and a body that radiated heat unlike anything I had ever experienced.

A shiver went through me. A very pleasurable shiver, especially as I recalled Kingsley's skillet-sized hands on my body. His touch, his expert touch, had sent shockwaves through me in more ways than one.

But as I stood there in the shower, as the water did its damned best to penetrate my eternal cold, I thought of another man.

Aaron Parker. Aka Fang.

The heat had worked deep into my skin, and as I stood there under the powerful spray, I reached behind me and turned the temperature even higher. Anyone else would have yelped. Anyone else would have leaped from the shower as surely as if being dropped into a boiling cauldron.

But I only moaned with pleasure.

After having drinks with Aaron, he had walked me back to my van where we had stood together awkwardly. He wanted to kiss me. He wanted to do a lot more to me, too. His thoughts were as clear as a bell, although anyone with a half a brain could have read his body language. I reminded him that I had a lot to digest. I reminded him that he had been aware of me for a lot longer than I had been aware of him. This needed to sink in. I had to sort through my feelings and emotions....

And that's when he kissed me.

He kissed me long and hard and although I had nearly pushed him back—hell, he was lucky he didn't go flying into the trunk of a nearby tree—I decided I liked his kiss. There had been a crazy hunger to him.

Or maybe he was just crazy.

His lips covered mine and I knew he wanted to bite me, or at least use his teeth. To nibble, to bite. To draw blood. When he got too aggressive, I pulled back. He apologized, and then went back to chewing on my lower face.

Never had I been kissed like that before.

Never. And never did I expect to be kissed like that again.

The shower spray felt so damn good. Too good. I could stand there all night. I could probably do other things in there all night, too. After all, I had recently discovered that I could experience something very pleasurable. Something I had thought was lost to me.

That thought alone sent a shiver through me.

I pushed it away and turned off the shower. There was work to be done. There was a little girl scared and alone and living with a monster.

And with images of Fang whispering goodbye in my ear, I got dressed and headed for my office at the back of the house.

Chapter Ten

I was scouring over internet leads, scanning heartbreaking article after heartbreaking article, when my cell phone rang. It was Chad.

"Hey, Sunshine," he said.

"It never gets old, does it?"

Chad was, of course, poking fun of my "condition". A condition called *xeroderma pigmentosum*, which was what most of the world thought I had. Believe it or not, I didn't run around telling people I was a vampire.

"Probably not ever," he said. "Besides, I'm your ex-partner. I can get away with goofing on you. Kind of like an older brother."

"A stupid-face older brother."

"Clever Sam. Anyway, I have news on Maddie."

I sat up. "Talk to me."

"Three months ago a mother and daughter went

missing. Lauren and Madison Monk."

I exhaled and squeezed the phone tighter. "Go on."

"The mother was a known user and prostitute and probably not a very good mother, either. The daughter was born into a mess. The mother would often disappear with boyfriends and drug dealers, bringing her daughter along with her. Some seedy shit going on here, Sam. No one reported them missing for many weeks, and she spent so much time with so many different shady characters, that it's nearly impossible to pinpoint where she was staying or who had seen her last."

"Someone knows," I said.

"Sure, but we're talking about the lowest of the lowlifes, Sam. Folks who break laws every hour on the hour. No one is talking."

"Who's working the case?"

"Fullerton Police Missing Persons Unit ."

"The name of the officer?"

He told me and I wrote it down. When finished, I said, "I think the missing person has turned into a murder and kidnapping."

"You'll hear no argument from me, Sam."

"Thank you, Chad."

"We're working on something big over here, but I'll help you when I can."

"I know; thank you. How's Monica?" I asked, referring to my client of just a few weeks ago. Chad, who had taken over partial bodyguard duties for me, had been smitten by her instantly.

"Beautiful as ever; I love her."

"Just don't smother her, for Christ's sake. Give her space."

"I'll give her whatever she wants."

"Oh, brother."

We hung up and I considered my options. Without the case file, there was really nothing I could do tonight. Tomorrow I would check in with the Fullerton P.D. For now, though, I quickly scanned my files and notes, doing a global search for the name Lauren Monk. Nothing came up. That didn't mean I hadn't come across her at some point, just that the name hadn't made it to any of my files or notes. Of course, that's if I had ever worked with her or come into contact with her in the first place.

Well, she had my number somehow.

Or, at least, *someone* had it.

I was sitting back and thinking about little Maddie and her little voice when I sensed a presence behind me. I turned and found Anthony standing there and looking miserable. "What's wrong, booger butt," I asked, waving him over.

"I don't feel good, Mommy."

"Hey, you're already suspended for a day, honey. You don't have to fake being sick." But I knew he wasn't faking it. My boy looked miserable and I could feel the palpable waves of heat coming off his body.

"But I'm not faking it, Mommy. I swear."

I put a hand on his forehead. The kid was burning up. He flinched at my icy touch. No surprise there. The dichotomy between hot and cold was probably startling.

He climbed up onto my lap and nuzzled his burning face into my neck, and as he did so, alarm bells went off inside me. They rang loud and clear.

Something was very wrong.

Chapter Eleven

I lay by Anthony's side for many hours, lightly running my fingers through his fine hair, periodically checking his fever with my palm. His cheek was clammy and frighteningly hot. His breathing was even, although I detected a slight rattle in his chest. Every now and then from his sleep he would cough wetly.

Something's wrong.

Or maybe I'm just worrying too much. He's just sick. A fever. Perhaps the flu.

The electrified air around my son was agitated, the glowing streaks buzzing like so many bees around a hive. I held my son closer and listened to his heartbeat; it beat strong and steady. I monitored his breathing, too, and was certain that, as the hours passed, his breathing was growing more ragged.

Hours later, I kissed him on his forehead and headed out into the living room. Tammy was snoring lightly with the TV playing quietly. An infomercial selling an electric wheelchair was on. The old guy cruising on it never looked happier. I doubted it.

I clicked off the TV and bent down. She was ten years old and weighed nearly as much as I did, that didn't stop me from scooping her up easily and cradling her in my arms like a baby. Her body was warm, but not alarmingly so. Unlike Anthony. I held her close to me and buried my nose in her hair, inhaling deeply. She smelled of strawberries. Again, unlike Anthony, who had smelled of sweat.

I stood there briefly in the living room, holding my daughter effortlessly while she mewed slightly in her sleep.

Somewhere out there was a little girl named Maddie who would never feel her mother nuzzle against her again. A little girl who knew only fear and perhaps pain. A little girl with the tiniest voice I had ever heard.

With my face still mostly buried in my daughter's hair, I carried her into her bedroom and eased her carefully down into bed. I pulled the covers up over her and kissed her warm forehead, and then wiped a tear off her cheek.

It had, of course, been my tear.

Chapter Twelve

You there, Fang?

It was late. Or early. Take your pick. Creatures of the night often get this distinction wrong. Anyway, I knew I would be waking Fang up, but I needed to talk.

I waited in front of my laptop for a few minutes with no response. I checked the time. Nearly 4:30 in the morning. Fang had worked tonight, I knew, which meant he would have gotten off at two-ish.

You're sleeping, I'm sure, I wrote in the IM screen. Years ago, Fang and I had met online in a community vampire room. I had been curious and lonely. Fang had not only landed a friend, but the real deal. A true bloodsucker.

Fang had entered my life when I needed him the most. Funny how life is like that. He was my outlet. My source of information, too, since he was knowledgeable in all things vampiric. We had bonded in ways I never thought possible, and I had revealed my deepest secrets. Fang knew everything.

And now I knew a lot more about him, too.

Fang was a killer. By my count, he had murdered three people. How many more after his jailbreak, I didn't know. I hoped none.

He had stalked me these past few years. Writing down clues. Saving our IM entries. That means he had confession after confession of my vampirism on record. Stored somewhere. I trusted Fang, but I wasn't sure what to think about this. He was certainly in a position to blackmail me, if he so chose, but I knew he wouldn't. I knew, and yes, *sensed*, that his interest in me stemmed from two sources: his love for vampires...and his love for me.

A strange day today, I wrote. *I thought of you often, I'll admit. And the most prevalent thought was: I kissed Fang! Do you mind if I still call you Fang? I kind of like it when you call me Moon Dance. Coming from you. it just feels right. It feels secretive, too, like spies, and these are our code names. I like that. I think everyone in life should have a code name. I won't mention your real name here, but I definitely don't see you as an Eli, either. You are Fang to me. Always Fang.*

I paused and reached for a pack of cigarettes sitting next to my computer. Recently I'd discovered that I could smoke. I don't recommend this to anyone but vampires, since smokes can't kill us. There are precious few things that I can ingest into my body without cramping up in pain, and smoking is one of them.

I'll take what I can get.

I lit up and exhaled a long plume of roiling gray smoke. The smoke cloud hovered briefly in front of me, then dissipated, and with the cigarette hanging from the corner of my mouth, I continued typing:

I'm not sure about the kiss. I'm not sure about anything, really. You know that I'm kind of involved with the attorney. He and I had a moment last week that I will never forget, although I won't go into it in any detail here. Let's just say it's hard for a woman to forget an experience like that (sorry if that hurts your feelings). But it's also hard for me to forget our kiss last night. So, tell me, what was it like to kiss a vampire? I'm sure my lips were cold. I'm sure my breath was cold, too. Isn't that a turn-off?

I was babbling, I knew, but these were thoughts that had been plaguing through my mind for years, and since my relationship with Fang had gone to another level, a physical level, I could ask him these questions.

I continued: *It was a turn-off for my husband. Once he vomited. No joke. He tried to lie about it, but I heard him retch and could smell the vomit on his breath. It's always nice when your husband vomits when making love to you. That was early on in my vampirism, of course. He never touched me again. Well, not in an intimate way. I never touched me, either. Transference, I believe the psychologists call it. I was unlovable in his eyes and so therefore I was unlovable in my own eyes. Yes, I know, I put too much weight into what he thought, but what was I supposed to do? I didn't know what was happening to me. Everything was all so new. His love meant everything to me. I needed it so bad and he wasn't there for me.*

I stopped writing and sat back. Ashes from my cigarette dropped onto my blouse. I always forgot to tap off the ashes. Smoking was still new to me. I wasn't sure how much I liked it, but it was at least nice to do something with my hands.

I guess I'm here to tell you that I don't want to lose what we have, Fang. But I'm not saying no to anything more, either. I guess I'm just not in any place to make decisions right now...and now my poor son is sick, and every alarm bell I have is ringing loudly. Something is wrong with him, Fang. But maybe that's just me worrying. Just a mom worrying.

I dashed out the last of the cigarette and looked at the blocks of words that filled the IM screen. Fang would have some reading to do once he woke up.

The sun was coming. I could feel it. A deep tiredness was setting in and I stumbled to my room where my shades were always drawn tight, and collapsed in sleep.

The sleep of the dead. Or undead.

Chapter Thirteen

I need an alarm clock—a very *loud* alarm clock —if I want to awaken any time before sunset. Left to my own devices, I awaken naturally just moments before the sun actually sets.

It's a nice system...unless you have kids.

It's very rare that I awaken on my own. But I did so now, and I awakened to find my son sleeping next to me. It was noonish. He had come in here on his own, to sleep next to his mommy. I wrapped my arms around his burning body and pulled him in close, feeling his forehead and was profoundly relieved that he didn't seem as hot.

Then again, I was barely cognizant. I was hardly in a place to make any sort of expert mommy inspections. Still, he seemed cooler and he was sleeping contentedly next to me.

As I fell back into my dreamless sleep, I

probably should have realized my son barely stirred, if at all.

***

My alarm went off at 2:00 p.m., my normal time to get up and get ready to pick up my kids.

As consciousness grudgingly returned, I listened to my son's even breathing next to me. Even, yet shallow. I turned on my side and touched his cheek. Shit. He was burning up again. Not quite as hot as last night, but my little boy was clearly sick.

I lay there for as long as I dared, alternately running my fingers through his hair and lightly touching his cheeks. He had my dark hair and Danny's broad-cheekboned looks. He had my long eyelashes, of which his sister was eternally jealous.

Finally I slipped out of bed and checked my email. Nothing of importance, although it did appear that I had been hand-picked to help a wealthy and desperate gentleman from Nigeria transfer his funds to the United States. His plan was genius: He would send me a whopper of a check, and I would send him a much smaller check in return. And get this: I get to keep the difference. Boy, what could go wrong with *that* idea?

I then spotted something blinking in the lower right-hand corner of my screen. An instant message from Fang. I *squee'd* and eagerly clicked on it. I might have gasped, too, and my heart definitely slammed hard against my third or fourth rib bone. Funny, I never reacted like this to Fang before.

His message was simple and to the point and it brought a big smile to my face:

I dreamed about you, Moon Dance. I always dream about you.

Smiling like a goofball, I quickly threw on a pair of jeans and a long-sleeved shirt. These days, I had quite the array of long-sleeved shirts. My day shirts, as I thought of them. My night attire was cuter. But my daytime wardrobe was all about survival...and staying out of the sun as much as possible.

Anyway, I slathered my hands and cheeks and neck with my heavy-duty sunblock, grabbed one of my many sunhats, carefully scooped my son up off my bed, and headed out the front door.

I dashed across the front yard, which never felt hotter. I threw open the garage door with a quick flick of my hand and plunged into the merciful shadows. Once there, I gasped and caught my breath.

My son barely stirred. He murmured "Mommy" and continued sleeping. I next buckled him into the back seat and wadded up the van's emergency blanket for a pillow.

And with the window shades pulled down, I backed up into the sunlight, and a few minutes later I was picking up my daughter. A few minutes after that I was at the Urgent Care, with my son in my arms.

Chapter Fourteen

It was four hours later and I was sitting in Detective Sherbet's office. Mary Lou, my sister, was watching the kids; in particular, keeping an eye on Anthony.

"Is everything okay?" asked Sherbet. He was sitting behind his desk and watching me curiously. He always watched me curiously.

I wanted to make a joke about how odd it was seeing Sherbet without a donut in his hand, but I just wasn't up to it. Instead, I said, "My son's sick."

Sherbet sat forward. He was a father who loved his own son. A son who was as effeminate as Sherbet was masculine. And Sherbet was as masculine as they come. Thick hair covered his forearms and the back of his hands. The hair was mostly gray. His belly pushed hard against his white dress shirt, putting a lot of pressure on the center buttons. In fact, the third button from the bottom was slightly frayed.

It's gonna blow, I thought.

The arm hair and rotund belly looked oddly appealing on Sherbet. Really, he was a man who had no business being thin. His body frame was built to hold the extra weight, and he did so in a sexy way. I always figured that if I was twenty years older I would have a serious crush on the man. I must not be the only one, since his own wife had to be pretty young to have a child still in elementary school. A child who, according to Sherbet, was on the fast track to homosexuality. A child who was forcing my detective friend to open his heart and mind in ways he never had before.

"So what do the doctors say?" he asked.

I shrugged. "Apparently the flu's going around. They told me not to worry."

"You're not doing a very good job of it, kiddo."

I shrugged. "Mostly, I'm worried your button is gonna blow and take out my eye."

He looked down at his belly. And now that I looked again, I was certain I could see the faint outline of a jelly stain. A jelly donut stain.

He nodded. "Okay, I get it. You don't want to talk about it."

"Not really," I said.

"And to deflect talk about your son, you choose instead to talk about my belly."

"It's quite a belly."

"I like my belly."

"I never said it was a bad belly."

He drummed his thick fingers on the wide desk. His fingernails were perfectly squared and seemed almost as thick as my own supernaturally thick nails.

"Can we stop talking about my belly?" he asked. "Besides, I don't think cops are supposed to say *belly*."

"And yet you've now said it four times."

He shook his head. "Don't worry about your boy, Sam. He'll be fine."

I nodded and wished I could believe him. Sherbet asked why I was here, and warned me from saying anything about his belly. I told him about Maddie and what my ex-partner had turned up. Sherbet listened quietly, and when I was finished he reached over and typed something on his keyboard. By typing, I mean he hunted and pecked slowly with his big sausage-like fingers.

"Hanner's working the case," he said.

"May I speak with him?"

"Her. Rachel Hanner. Hang on."

He got up from behind his desk, and as he did so, one of his knees popped so loudly that I nearly took cover. Sherbet looked slightly embarrassed. "Don't say a word," he cautioned.

"Wouldn't dream of it," I smirked.

He returned a moment later with a young woman with perfect milky skin. She was also damn pretty, and I fought an overwhelming desire to hate her. She nodded at me pleasantly but didn't shake my hand.

Bitch, although I was secretly relieved. Shaking hands always followed a small bit of stress for me.

Sherbet asked her to sit and she did so next to me. Sherbet next asked me to retell my story and I did so, reciting it nearly word for word. These days, my memory seemed sharper and sharper. I had no idea what to attribute that to, but I wasn't complaining.

When I was finished, Hanner nodded once and turned and looked at me. Her movements were economical and precise. She seemed like a well-oiled—and quite beautiful—machine. Her blond hair was pulled back tightly, revealing a smooth sweep of forehead. Her eyes were impossibly big, and most guys probably would have had the hots for her if she didn't project such a fiercely calm and professional presence.

"I can't imagine that a child knows how to block caller ID," she said when I was finished. Her voice had a hint of an accent. Or maybe, for once, I was simply hearing perfectly enunciated English.

"Which is why I figured the phone had the block already programmed in."

She nodded. "A reasonable assumption. Is your business number a toll free number, Samantha?"

"At the time of the call, no."

"But you have it now?"

"Better. Just before coming here I added another feature to my phone, called Trap Call."

"I'm not following," said Sherbet.

No surprise there. Sherbet was an old-school homicide detective and probably not up to date on some of the modern tracing technology. Conversely, private investigators were almost always up on such new gadgets. New gadgets gave us an edge over our competitors. Including the police. Of course, having a freaky sixth sense was a hell of an advantage, too. He said, "And what does that do?"

"It's a call forwarding service," I said, "When a blocked call comes through, I forward it to Trap Call and their toll-free line. The caller's ID shows up on their end, and Trap Call relays the information to me. Within seconds."

Sherbet looked at Murphy. "This make sense to you?"

"Perfectly."

"Good enough. So we wait for the next call, then?" he said.

I nodded. "If it comes. Until then, I would like to assist you on this case."

"Do you have a paying client?" asked Sherbet.

"No."

Sherbet looked at Hanner. "Could you use the help?"

"More than you know," she answered.

He looked back at me. "You can help. Unofficially, of course."

"Of course."

Sherbet asked Hanner to leave the case file with him and she obliged. She smiled at me, nodded at Sherbet, and left.

The detective touched the file on his desk, and said, "I'm going to get some coffee. Maybe a donut. Okay, definitely a donut. I'll be gone for about ten minutes. You are not to look at this official police file, and you are most definitely not to copy them on the convenient copy machine in the corner of my office."

"Yes, sir."

He set the file down in front of me, and when he left to get his coffee and donut, I quickly made a copy of the file. I slipped my copy in my purse and returned the original to its folder.

When Sherbet returned with his coffee and a fresh jelly stain, he calmly picked up the file and dropped it in the "Out" box at the corner of his desk.

"I trust you didn't look at the file," he said.

"Wouldn't dream of it, sir."

"So what's your first step?" he asked.

"First, I'm going to read a file I most certainly didn't copy. And second, then I'm going to do what I do best."

"Drive to soccer games in your minivan?"

"Hey, I only do that twice a week."

"Go on."

I said, "I'm going to relentlessly look for this little girl until I find her, using whatever means I have at my disposal."

"All of them legal, of course."

"Of course," I said.

Sherbet sipped his coffee, and promptly

splashed some down his shirt. He briefly glanced at it but he really didn't seem to care, truth be known. Okay, now *that* is manly.

He said, "And don't think I've forgotten about our little talk, Samantha."

Sherbet was referring to the recent supernatural activity happening in his town. Minor stuff, really. Just a werewolf sighting or two. Maybe a grave robbery. Maybe.

"I haven't, Detective. It's just that now isn't a good time."

He was nodding. "When your son's better and you have a little time, we're going to talk."

"Of course," I said, and got up. "I can find my way out."

I left him staring after me, with his coffee and jelly donut stains.

Chapter Fifteen

I called my sister Mary Lou, and she told me that Anthony was sleeping peacefully. I breathed a sigh of relief.

"I think I just heard you breathe an actual sigh of relief," said Mary Lou.

"Wouldn't you?"

"He's going to be fine, Sam. You worry too much."

"It's my job to worry too much," I said.

"And it's my job to call you on it."

I asked her to watch him a little longer and she said she was planning on staying the night. Her own children were at home with their dad, which made me briefly envious. Hey, I'm only human.

I think.

Having Danny around had made my job infinitely easier. That is, until he started coming home later and later—and reeking of perfume. Then my life wasn't easier. Then it had been a living hell.

I thanked her and clicked off and checked the time on my dash. It was going to be a tight squeeze but I should make it to my meeting on time.

I took Chapman Avenue to the 57 Freeway. From there, I joined a sea of other cars and headed south. Luckily, this sea was moving at a decent clip, and soon I was going east on the 22, where I exited at Main Street. From there, I headed south, passing one of Orange County's greatest edifices: The Main Place Mall, whose postmodern glass-and-metal facade sparkled in the last light of the day like a giant beacon to desperate housewives with too much money and a penchant for giant-sized cinnamon rolls.

Somehow, I managed to resist the urge to spend thirty minutes looking for parking and pay twice the going rate for anything. Of course, I was dead broke and I doubted Cinnabons served chilled hemoglobin.

The broke part was why I was taking this meeting.

A few blocks later, I turned into the Wharton Museum parking lot. As I did so, the sun finally set behind a horizon cluttered with apartment buildings and old homes. I stepped out of my minivan and inhaled the warm dusk air and felt more alive than I ever did when I was human.

God, I felt so strong. So powerful.

I swept through a long, arched tunnel full of hanging vines, past the sitting area of an outdoor cafe, nodded at a large tour group leaving the museum, and stepped inside Orange County's only significant cultural museum.

At the front desk, a young docent smiled brightly at me. "I'm sorry, ma'am, but we're closed." She seemed profoundly relieved that they were closed. Perhaps today had been a particularly difficult day at the museum. I suspected I knew why. In fact, I knew the reason why.

I told her who I was and why I was here. Somehow, she managed to contain her excitement. She made a call, nodded, and a moment later led me down a hallway lined with offices and cubicles. Or perhaps these weren't offices and cubicles. Maybe this was some weird, hip, modernistic "Cubicles as Art" exhibit.

Or not.

I was led to the last office on the left, where a tall woman with a vigorous handshake greeted me and showed me to a guest chair in front of her desk.

I sat and she sat, and after a short exchange of pleasantries, she got right to the point. "As you know, Ms. Moon, we had a robbery here last night."

"Yes, you mentioned that over the phone. I'm sorry to hear it."

Her name was Ms. Dickens. Yes, that's how she introduced herself to me on the phone and even now in person. So, on that note, I introduced myself as Ms. Moon, and she seemed perfectly at ease with that. I wasn't at ease with it. I mean, c'mon.

Anyway, *Ms.* Dickens wore a very old-fashioned business suit and seemed about twenty years older than I suspected she really was. She was a seventy-year-old woman trapped in a fifty-year-old's body.

She said, "I assure you, so am I. The police have been called, of course. And as far as they can tell it was an inside job. The police, however, don't seem to grasp the nature of the crime or the importance of the stolen artifact. I fear that our case will be forgotten by the overworked Santa Ana Police Department."

I made sympathetic noises. Truth was, overworked police departments are what kept many private eyes in business. Had police departments been adequately staffed, I would have been relegated to doing background searches and cheating spouse cases. Background cases were fine, and were easy money, but I avoided cheating spouse cases at all costs. I hated hearing the rotten cheating stories, and I hated being involved in the painful drama.

Not to mention, I tended to want to strangle all the cheating men. I wonder why?

Not to mention, I was a trained federal agent. I was above cheating spouse cases...unless, of course, I needed money.

Anyway, I asked what had been stolen, since Ms. Dickens had been vague on the phone. "A single item," she answered. "A crystal egg sculpture from the Harold Van Pelt collection."

Harold Van Pelt, apparently, was a world-class

gem photographer. But what wasn't so well-known was that he had become, over the course of 35 years, a master gemstone carver. Apparently, he had perfected the art of taking a solid block of quartz and turning it into hollowed vases or, in this case, a hollowed egg. The Wharton was the first museum to showcase his work.

"The quartz is cut so paper thin and polished so perfectly that it is as clear as glass. How he does it, I have no clue."

"Well, like they always say, just carve away anything that doesn't look like a crystal egg, right?"

She stared at me. "I'm sure there's more to it than that, Ms. Moon." I was fairly certain that if she had a ruler, she would have rapped my knuckles with it.

"Why do the police think this was an inside job?" I asked.

"They haven't said."

"Which makes sense," I said. "If it was an inside job."

Ms. Dickens tilted her head to one side. "Are you implying that I'm a suspect, Ms. Moon?"

"Oh, it's much too soon for me to imply that," I said, smiling brightly.

Not to mention I wasn't getting a negative feel from Ms. Dickens; meaning, she checked out clean to my sixth sense. That is, if it was to be relied upon.

Brightly or not, Ms. Dickens didn't like the direction this conversation was going. I didn't, either, for that matter. I needed the job and I needed her retainer check. Badly. The last thing I needed to do was offend the lady. There was always time to offend her later.

The curator unpursed her lips. She was, after all, a reasonable woman. Or so I hoped. She said, "If this was an inside job, then I suppose everyone here is indeed a potential suspect. Me included."

"Some people are less suspect than others," I added.

"You have a job to do," she said, which was encouraging. "And part of that job is getting answers. I get it."

"Thank you," I said.

"Well, you certainly seem capable, Ms. Moon. I called your references. In particular, your boss at HUD. Earl, I believe his name was. Anyway, he assures me you are very professional and reliable. I think he used the word *spunky*."

I had worked at HUD for a number of years before my attack rendered me into something...very different. After the attack, I had been forced to quit my job and work the night shift as a private eye. The transition from a federal investigator to a private investigator had been an easy one, although I missed the camaraderie of a partner and the massive resources of the federal government. Luckily, or perhaps, smartly, I retained my friendships with most people in the agency, and often they gave me access to their super-cool computers.

"Earl always thought highly of me," I said.

"He also said you were forced to quit suddenly because of a rare skin disease." She tilted her head down, studying me over her bifocals. "Could you expand on that?"

"It's a rare disease that I have under control. Mostly, I have to stay out of the sun and away from McDonald's heating lamps."

"I see some of that spunkiness coming through."

"You caught me."

"Will your condition affect your performance?"

"No, ma'am, although I tend to work nights, as we've already discussed over the phone."

"Working nights is fine with us. We don't need any more distractions during the day. And besides, the theft occurred at night, too. Maybe there's something to that."

"Maybe," I said. *Sheesh, everyone's a detective.* "Is there a special crew that works the night shift?"

"Security crew, yes. I will introduce you to some of them shortly." Ms. Dickens paused and held my gaze. "I need to underline the importance of this investigation, Ms. Moon. We are a respectable, although small, cultural museum. We've had everything from rare Egyptian treasures to paintings by Van Gogh. A theft like this could shatter our international image and keep the popular exhibits away. Ms. Moon, the Wharton Museum is slowly making a name for itself as a world class cultural museum. We need all the help we can get, and we will pay big if you can recover the crystal egg."

We discussed exactly how big, and it was all I could do to keep my mouth from dropping open. We next discussed a retainer fee, and she paid it without blinking, writing me a company check. The retainer fee would pay my mortgage for the next three months, and maybe a car payment or two.

Things were looking up.

She gave me a quick tour and then we shook hands and I left the way I had come, passing more live exhibits of mankind in his natural working habitat.

Or perhaps they were just offices and cubicles.

Chapter Sixteen

I called Mary Lou and got the rundown.

Anthony was awake and seemed to be holding steady. No real progress, but no relapse either. Still, my gut churned. When I thought about my son, I saw something dark around him. The brightness and vitality that surrounded him was gone.

I desperately feared what that darkness could mean.

To get my thoughts off my son, I headed over to Zov's bistro in Costa Mesa, where I ordered a rare steak and a glass of white wine. The upscale Mediterranean restaurant was the epitome of hip, and I even noticed Orange County's bestselling writer sitting just a few tables down. He looked serious. Maybe he was plotting his next thriller. I wondered if he could sense that a real live vampire was sitting just a few tables away.

While I waited, I plunged into Maddie's police

file, reading every note and witness statement.

I knew I should be with my son, and I would be soon, but for now there was a little girl missing, and she had made it very personal by calling me.

By calling me, even accidentally, she had assured herself of one thing: a private investigating psychic vampire mommy who was going to find her.

No matter what.

My food arrived quickly. The nice thing about ordering steaks rare is that they don't take long to cook. And as I read from the folder, I discreetly used a spoon to slurp the blood that had pooled around the meat. I also cut the meat up without actually eating it. I scattered the chunks around my plate, hiding some under my salad. I felt like a kid hiding her food.

The blood was wonderful and satisfied some of my craving, although I would need more later. And when I had drained the meat dry, I moved on to the glass of white wine. When the wine was done, I was done reading the police report, too.

Granted, there wasn't much to go on, but I had a few leads. I paid my bill, glanced a final time at the waiter—who was now openly staring at me— and left Zov's Bistro.

I had a girl to find.

Chapter Seventeen

I was driving down the 57 Freeway when my cell rang. I glanced down at it. Kingsley Fulcrum, a one-time client of mine who had turned into something more than a client.

A few weeks ago we had been intimate, an experience that had rocked my world, and shortly after that I was reminded of what a scumbag he could be. Kingsley was a defense attorney. A very high profile and rich defense attorney. He got paid the big bucks to get people out of jail. As far as I could tell, the man had no moral compass. Killer or not, if the price was right, he would do his damnedest to get you to walk.

Did I still care for the big lug? Yeah, I did. Did the thought of him in bed turn me on more than I cared to admit? Sweet Jesus, it did. Did the fact that he had shown up in my hotel room a week or so ago as a fully morphed werewolf, dripping blood and reeking of death, scare the shit out of me? Hell, yeah.

I clicked on, resisting the urge to sing "Werewolves of London" yet again. When your boy is sick and you're looking for a kidnapped girl, well, your humor is the first to go.

"What, no 'Werewolves of London'? No 'Arooo'? You're losing your touch, Sam."

"It's not a good time, Kingsley."

"So serious. Okay, have it your way. Where will you be in about an hour?"

"My best guess? In the face of some crackhead punk."

"A shakedown. Sounds exciting. Tell me about it."

I did. I also told him about my son.

"Yeah, you've had a rough few days. How's your son now?"

"Sleeping last I heard."

"But you're still worried."

"More than you know." I paused, gathered my wits, and plunged on. "I see death around him, Kingsley."

"Death?"

"A blackness. A coldness. A sort of dark halo that surrounds his body. I'm totally freaked out."

Kingsley was silent for a heartbeat or two. "He'll be fine, Sam."

But I heard it in his voice. I heard the doubt.

"You don't believe that," I said. Tears suddenly blurred my eyes. I was having a hard time keeping the van in the center of the lane. "And don't deny it."

"Sam, I don't know anything, okay? I'm not psychic. My kind are not traditionally psychic."

"But my kind is?"

"Often. And you seem to be growing more psychic by the day."

"What do you know of the black halo? Tell me. Please."

"I know very little, Sam."

A nearly overwhelming sense of panic gripped me. "But you know it's not good."

"I know nothing, Sam. Look, now is not a good time to talk about this. You're driving. You're helping this little girl. Let's meet for drinks later this week, okay?"

"Okay," I said.

"Good. And Sam?"

"Yes?"

"I care about you deeply. Your family, too. Everything will be okay. I promise."

I broke down, crying hard, and clicked off.

Chapter Eighteen

I pulled up to a squalid house in Buena Park, about a mile north of Knott's Berry Farm.

I sat in my minivan for a few minutes and took in the scene. Apartments across the street. A gang of Hispanic males a block away to the west. They were smoking and drinking and listening to music. The music pumped from a four-door sedan whose front end was hydraulically propped up off the ground two or three feet. The car looked ridiculous and cool at the same time. I wasn't sure which. The gang ignored my van, which was probably a good idea. The last time I had a run-in with a Latino gang someone had died.

And gotten himself drained of blood, too.

The moon was obscured by a gauzy veil of clouds. The street had a mean feel to it. The area itself seemed malevolent, and I suspected this awareness was a result of my increased psychic abilities. I sensed death on this street. I sensed stabbings and robberies and harassment and fear. I sensed drug deals and drugs deals gone bad. I sensed a ramshackle attempt at organized crime. I sensed killers and victims. It was all here, infusing the air and the earth, the trees and the buildings. A calling card of hate for anyone sensitive enough to feel it. And I was sensitive enough. Perhaps too sensitive. The feeling was overwhelming. Energy crackled crazily through the air, too—and now that I knew what to look for, I saw many vague spirits walking among the living. Murder victims mostly. But some were lost souls, whose lives were taken by drug abuse or physical abuse.

It was into this environment of loss and despair and suffering that I stepped out of my minivan.

A low iron fence surrounded the property. The gate was topped with rusted iron spikes. The spikes were mostly rounded and probably wouldn't do much damage unless someone fell from a great height. The front gate was not locked and swung open on rusted hinges. As I moved across the front yard, I felt eyes on me from across the street. I had attracted the attention of the neighbors in the apartment building. No doubt watching from one of the windows.

I stepped up onto the cement porch, which was cracked and flaked with peeling paint. I paused a moment, getting a feel for the house. Someone was inside, I knew that much. I could hear a TV on somewhere. The house itself was drenched in so much tragedy that it was a beehive of bad vibes, depression and anything else negative.

More than anything, the house was the last known residence of Lauren Monk and her daughter Maddie. I shook my head. What a place to raise a little girl.

Granted, I doubted there was much "raising" going on here. *Existing* was more like it.

I knocked on the door loudly. The door was made of metal and seemed better suited in a parking garage stairwell. There were dents in the door, about waist high. Someone had tried to kick it in at some point. Maybe many points. I looked around the metal frame. As far as I could tell, they weren't successful. The door and frame had held firm.

The TV continued to blare. A distant siren wailed behind me. Down the street someone laughed and others followed suit. I knocked again, and again.

No response.

I stepped back, lifted my foot, and kicked the door in.

Chapter Nineteen

The door swung violently back, slamming hard into the wall behind it, so hard that the doorknob punctured the drywall. It stayed open like that as I stepped in. Unless someone was brandishing a stake or silver-tipped arrows, I wasn't too concerned about what was waiting for me on the other side. Sure, a bullet to the chest probably would hurt like hell, and no doubt ruin my blouse, but gone are the days where I worried much about my own physical safety.

I found myself standing in a living room. Or a toxic bio-hazard. Take your pick. The long clump of trash to my right was probably a couch. The rectangular clump in front of it was probably a coffee table. Everything from shopping bags to clothing to pizza boxes were everywhere. Including used heroin needles. Everywhere. Hundreds of them.

I stepped over broken glass and empty beer cans and a McDonald's Happy Meal. I moved through the living room and into a kitchen that hadn't been used as a kitchen in some time.

Instead, it was being used as a meth lab.

There were bottles and jars with rubber tubing. There were stripped-down lithium batteries piled on tables. Paint thinner and starter fluid containers lined the floors. Empty packets of cold tablets, no doubt containing pseudoephedrine, were piled on the tables and counters. Also on the tables were jars containing clear liquid with red and white bottom layers. Ether and ammonia wafted from them. Propane tanks were everywhere. Okay, the propane tanks made me a little nervous.

There was a strong smell of something else. And it was coming from the next room. I knew that smell. Any cop or agent would know that smell.

I moved through the kitchen and down a short hallway. I had sensed someone else in the house, but what I had not sensed was whether or not that someone was alive or dead.

At the far end of the hallway, in a room to the right, a TV was on and a man wearing boxer shorts was lying face down in a pool of blood. In death, he had made an unholy mess of himself, but that did not stop me from checking him out.

I rolled him over. Blood stained the mattress. Probably all the way through and to the bed springs below. I counted five shots to the chest. I wrinkled my nose, although wrinkling did little against what was wafting up from him.

I did a quick examination. White male in his early fifties. Dead for less than 24-hours, give or take a half a day. Heavy set. No indication of a fight. The body already in full rigor mortis. Face bright crimson where the blood had settled like oil at the bottom of an oil pan.

I eased him back down.

Years ago such a scene might have turned my stomach. I might have picked a quiet spot behind the house to vomit, careful not to disrupt a crime scene. Now, not so much. I had seen many dead bodies in my time, certainly, but there was something else going on. Something that worried me. I should care more about death, about the loss of life. But I didn't.

Death no longer bothered me. Didn't faze me. I felt no emotion or concern or anything.

It was just death.

The natural order of things.

I wasn't always this way, but something had changed inside of me, and I think I knew what that something was.

I was becoming less human...and that scared the shit out of me.

I spent the next twenty minutes carefully picking through the house, looking for any clues that might help me find little Maddie, but nothing stood out. No Rolodexes filled with the names of drug kingpins. No computers or laptops. No cell phones. Nothing that seemed to indicate that a little girl had ever lived here.

Nothing, that is, except for the Happy Meal box.

I pulled out my cell phone and called Detective Sherbet.

Chapter Twenty

I spent the next two hours with Detective Sherbet and Detective Hanner. I gave them my statement, stood back and watched the preliminary crime scene investigation, and when all the fuss was over, I headed over to Heroes in Fullerton, where Fang worked.

As I walked up to Heroes' single door, a door which always somehow seemed to be slightly cracked open, I ran a hand through my thick hair and fought a sudden wave of nerves. I adjusted and readjusted my light leather jacket.

It was just after 1:00 a.m. when I stepped inside the bar. Heroes is filled with a lot of wooden beams and columns. The floor creaks when you walk across it, and more often than not, you will find a pool of spilled beer somewhere nearby, reflecting the muted track lighting above.

Aaron Parker, aka Eli something or other, aka

the American Vampire, aka Fang, was tending bar alone tonight. He was chatting with two guys in flannel shirts when he looked up and caught my eye. He smiled broadly. It was the same look he had always given me since being hired here months ago.

Since stalking me and taking this job.

I must have mentioned in one of my IMs to him that my sister frequented Heroes. Initially, I had thought I would be more careful than that, but I had let my guard down with Fang. And he had not only found out who I was, but had gotten a job at the very bar I frequented with my sister.

Creepy. And well, sweet, too.

Aaron Parker was clearly a nut. That much was certain. He was also a killer. But, more than anything, he was Fang. My Fang.

Maybe we're all nuts.

I saw now the hint of longing in his eyes. Saw the deep concern for me. Perhaps it was love. I never noticed it before. Or, if I did, I hadn't given it much attention. I had been a married woman until recently. Besides, maybe I thought he had been hamming it up for an extra big tip.

But I saw him differently now. In a new light, so to speak. The attention, the intent behind his gaze...all of it was for me.

I took in a small, sharp breath.

He smiled and unconsciously pulled back his upper lip. In that moment, in this lighting, I had a brief flashback to the disturbed teenage boy who seemed to relish pulling back his upper lip in the courtroom, the boy whose fanged smile had made front page headlines across the country.

That boy was a man now. And although he had some plastic surgery, appeared to have grown a foot or more and was sporting a beard, there was enough similarity to give me pause.

He's a killer, I thought. *A murderer.*

The tormented young man had grown into something beautiful, but that made him no less tormented or sick. I had not known Fang to be sick. Obsessive, certainly. But his advice had always been spot on, and his caring for me had been genuine. Or, at least, *seemed* genuine.

And his smile—that sexy, slightly awkward smile—seemed genuine, too. I walked up to the bar just as he reached for a bottle of white wine.

"Hello Sam," he said easily. The massive teeth that dangled from the leather strap around his neck clanked together with the sound of two thick beer mugs toasting. Clearly the rest of the world thought these were shark teeth. Or perhaps some other creature. Barracuda? Sasquatch?

"Hello Eli," I said, using his official name, although I sat at the far end of the mostly empty bar.

"We are so formal tonight," he said.

"*We* are still in shock from last night."

"We are?"

"Oh yes," I said.

"You never expected me to be so dashingly handsome, perhaps?"

"I didn't expect you to be a renowned fugitive."

He calmly cleaned a shot glass, as if he was just another bartender. "And does that bother you?"

"That you're a wanted man? That I'm cavorting with a known criminal?"

"Cavorting?"

"It's a word," I said.

He grinned easily and leaned across the counter, putting most of his weight on his palms. His two teeth hung freely from his neck like pale corpses twisting in the wind. "It's kind of a sexy word."

I looked away. I would have blushed if I could have. "I think you're taking it out of context."

"I prefer my context."

"Are you quite done?" I said. "I thought we were just friends."

"Just friends? After that kiss last night?"

"That kiss was your idea."

"I seem to recall you enthusiastically participating."

"Can we change the subject?" I said.

He grinned broadly. "Sure. Whatever would you like to talk about, my lady?"

I shrugged and sipped the white wine. Wine has no effect on me, but it's one of the few things, outside of hemoglobin, that I can drink like a regular person. Red wine not so much. Red wines contain tannins that upset my stomach. For someone who is supposedly immortal, my digestive system is hypersensitive.

I said, "I just want to talk to a friend."

"You know I'm your friend, Moon Dance."

"I like when you call me Moon Dance."

"I know. I read your epic IMs this morning when I woke up. Truth be known, I like it when you call me Fang, too."

"Fang and Moon Dance," I said, shaking my head. "We're weird."

"More than anyone could possibly know." He glanced around his mostly empty bar as any good bartender would, saw that his few patrons were content, and looked back at me. "Sorry I missed your IMs last night. I crashed as soon as I got home."

"No worries. It was late."

"It's difficult to keep up with your schedule, you know."

I laughed and set down the worthless wine. Who was I kidding? I wasn't normal. Why was I so concerned about looking normal?

Fang reached out and touched the back of my hand. His warm touch sent a shockwave of shivers up my arms and down my back. "You know," he said, "there is a way that you and I could have the same schedule."

"Oh?" I said, curious. "Would I need to get a second job here as a barback?"

"That's not what I meant, Moon Dance."

He continued touching me. His thumb lightly stroked the back of my hand. His fingers slipped under and caressed my palm. I shivered. Fang wasn't looking at me. I sensed his hesitation, and I sensed his insane desire.

Now Fang turned to me and our eyes met and I found myself looking deep into another person's soul for the first time in my life. Everything opened up to me. All his secrets. All his desires. All his wants and needs and hopes and dreams. And cravings. I gasped.

Fang gave me a lopsided smile.

"Yes, Moon Dance," he said. "Make me a vampire."

Chapter Twenty-one

It had been a long night.

When I got home, I discovered that everyone was sleeping in my bed, including little Anthony. I stood in the doorway of my bedroom, taking the scene in: Tammy on her back and snoring lightly. My sister in the middle and lying on her side with her palm resting lightly on Anthony's back.

A beautiful blue glow surrounded my daughter. The blue glow was interlaced with swatches of gold. The aura around my sister was a powerful orange, a contented color, a peaceful color.

There was no color around my son. There was only a deep blackness. It was as if he didn't exist at all. The light energy around him seemed to enter that black field and disappear. Like a black hole.

I rubbed my eyes and fought my tears. I slipped into some sweats and a tank top and slid into bed next to Anthony. I, too, rested my palm on his back.

His burning back.

***

I lay like that for a long time, waiting for the sun to rise, and when it did, I was out to the world.

Some hours later, I was awakened by my ringing cell phone. Generally, my ringing cell phone doesn't awaken me. But in the darkness of my deep sleep, a sleep where I seriously suspected I lay in a state of suspended animation somewhere between life and death—I had heard a shouting. Someone, somewhere had shouted my name.

It had been shocking enough to awaken me from my coma-like sleep.

Half-dead, I snatched the ringing phone off the nightstand and flipped it open, barely aware that it had said "Caller Unknown" on the faceplate. My son, I saw, was lying next to me...in a pool of sweat.

"Hello?" I said, instinctively reaching for my son and feeling his forehead. Burning up. My heart skip-hopped in my chest. Panic raced through me.

"Hi," said a tiny and familiar voice.

But I was too distracted with my son for the voice to fully register. Two seconds later, the voice sank in, and I snapped my head around as if someone had spoken next to me, rather than through my phone line.

"Maddie!" I gasped, practically squealing.

"Hi," she said again. Her voice, if anything,

sounded even smaller and fainter. I had an image of her covering her mouth as she spoke. This image came to me with crystal clarity and I suspected it was a psychic hit. Takes awhile to believe such hits are accurate...until you see enough evidence. I've seen the evidence now.

At that moment, a text message appeared on my phone. The call tracing had worked. A phone number was waiting for me. Maddie's number.

"Maddie," I gasped, trying to control myself. "Please, honey, can you tell me the name of the person you're with?"

"He's the bad man."

"Do you know his name, angel?"

I saw her shaking her head in my mind's eye. She didn't answer me, but I knew her answer: No, she didn't know.

"Honey, what does he look like?"

"He shot my mommy. He kilt her dead."

"I know, baby. Please can you tell me what he looks like?"

"Old."

Old to a five year old could be anything from nineteen to ninety. "Does he have gray hair?"

"None."

"No hair?"

"No hair," she said. "He eats too much."

"Good, honey. Good. Is he fat? Does he have a big belly?"

I sensed her nodding but she didn't answer. I also sensed that she didn't completely understand that I couldn't see her nod, that she thought she had answered my question. I had a fabulous connection with this little girl. Almost an immediate one, perhaps born of desperation. I had an idea.

"Honey," I said, "close your eyes."

"But why?"

"Please, just close your eyes."

There was a sound from somewhere and in my mind's eye I saw the little girl's head jerk up. Someone was coming.

"Please, honey, just close your eyes."

"The bad man is coming."

"Close them for one second."

"He's going to hurted me again."

"Please honey. Please. Do it for me. One time."

And she did. I knew she did, because I was instantly given a deeper access to her mind and memories and I saw an image of a room. A nice room. No, a beautiful room. A house? Condo? Apartment? I was having a hard time placing the interior. Whatever it was, it was epic. Where the hell was she? I didn't know. Through her window I saw something glittering brightly on the hillside. A desert hillside.

I saw something else. A black man. A bald black with an enormous stomach. He was standing over her and doing things that would be the death of him.

"He's coming!" she whispered over the phone, snapping me out of my reverie and out of her own memories.

"Okay, angel. Okay. Thank you, baby." I was crying now, but she would never know it. "Be strong, Maddie, for me, okay?"

"I scared."

"Be strong, angel. I'm coming for you soon. I swear."

"Okay," she said, "I strong."

I sensed a great presence near her, coming from somewhere behind her, and now her fear knew no end. As if my own, I felt her heart race faster than I had ever felt a heart race before.

"Go!" I said. "Go!"

Next I heard a scraping sound, perhaps her hand moving over the mouthpiece, and what she said next broke me into a million little pieces. She whispered: "I love you."

And then she hung up.

Chapter Twenty-two

I was at the Urgent Care again.

It was late afternoon and I was determined to get my son some help. No, I'd be damned if I wasn't going to get him some help. The gut-wrenching call from Maddie had sent me into a panicked frenzy with my own son.

As soon as I had hung up with her, as soon as I stopped hearing her precocious little voice telling me she loved me, I traced the call. Nothing was coming up. I called my ex-partner, Chad, and he ran the number through the Agency's database. The news was grim: The phone number belonged to an unregistered, throw-away cell phone.

Shit.

Next, I threw on my clothes and sunscreen, picked up my boy, and hit the road. He barely stirred in my arms or in the van.

It was still hours before I had to pick up Tammy. In the waiting room, with Anthony in my arms, I texted Danny and caught him up to date on the situation, asking him to pick Tammy up for me. His reply was immediate and curt: "Meetings all day; update me on Anthony ASAP."

Yes, he actually used a semi-colon. The piece of shit had enough time to find the semi-colon button but not enough time to help me.

My reply was equally curt: "Thanks for the help, asshole;;;;;"

Yes, complete with five semi-colons in a row.

Childish, certainly, but I didn't care. I needed help. I didn't need semi-colons.

The asshole.

I replayed Maddie's words again and again. As I did so, I rocked my son in my arms. It was mid-day and I felt weak and agitated and vulnerable. But even at my weakest, I was still stronger than I had any right to be.

The black man was bald. He was in his fifties. I saw him from Maddie's perspective, from her eyes. He was a big man. Often sweating. Odor wafted from his body.

I blocked some of the other images I had seen. I didn't need to dwell on those. Those images would tear my heart out.

I locked them away as best as I could.

But not his face. No. I would never forget his face.

I'm coming for you, asshole, I thought.

I had a strong connection to Maddie. Perhaps it was a connection out of necessity. Amazingly, her phone call had roused me from the deepest of sleeps. Trust me, no easy feat. That connection, I was certain, would lead me to her. Eventually.

Sooner rather than later.

My son stirred in my arms, moaning slightly, and then nuzzled deeper into the crook of my neck.

Where was that fucking doctor?

I haven't been sick in six years, except if you count the overwhelming fatigue I feel before the sun goes down. Vampire Fatigue Syndrome. Whatever. Anyway, I suspected I would never get sick again. I couldn't say the same for my kids.

Anthony wriggled in my arms and leaned back. He turned his sweating face toward me, opened his eyes. "Mommy?" he croaked.

The instant he said the word I heard another little voice in my head say something similar: "He kilt my mommy dead."

"Hey, baby," I said. I did my best to ignore the black halo around his angelic face.

"Where are we?"

"At the doctor's, honey."

He nodded. "I don't feel very good."

"I know, baby doll."

He continued staring at me even while I looked ahead and tried to be strong. He was so hot. I started rocking him slightly. I could feel the tears on my cheeks.

"Mommy?"

"Yes, sweetie?"

"I'm gonna die."

I stopped rocking and snapped my head down. "Why would you say that?"

"I dream that I go to heaven. I always dream it now. And he's waiting for me."

I think my heart stopped. "Who's waiting for you?"

Anthony actually smiled and reached up and touched my face. "You know, Mommy."

I was crying now. Openly crying and I couldn't stop myself. No, I didn't know who. God? Jesus? Krishna? Who was waiting for my son? *What was happening?*

"Don't cry, Mommy," he said. "He told me to be brave. He told me to be brave for you." He touched my cheek gently and I realized he was wiping away my tears. "I'm being brave for you, Mommy."

I pulled him into me and rocked faster and faster, and as I rocked, words tumbled out of me uncontrollably: "You're not dying. You're not dying. *You're not dying....*"

Chapter Twenty-three

The visit to the Urgent Care turned into something more than a visit. My son's fever was climbing. The doctor there examined my son's stomach and thyroid glands. He didn't like what he was seeing. I didn't either. My son had a rash on his belly that I had missed and his thyroid was swollen many millimeters. Blood samples were taken. My son never blinked when he was pricked with the many needles.

I impassively watched his blood being drawn.

The doctor left and I sat holding my son, who seemed to doze off and on. I rocked him gently and discovered I was humming a song to myself. I fought to remain calm but I couldn't. My lower jaw was shaking nearly uncontrollably. I had never felt so damned cold in my life, even while I held my burning son.

I rocked and hummed and prayed. The tears

came without saying.

An hour later, my son woke up laughing. Startled, I asked him what he was laughing about, and he told me that Jesus had told him a funny joke. He giggled again and went back to sleep.

I continued rocking.

The doctor came back. He had arranged for a bed at St. Jude Children's Research Hospital in Orange, which is where I now found myself an hour later.

The doctor who met me at the hospital smiled warmly and held my cold hands with a look of utter fascination. What he made of my cold hands, I didn't know or care. He did not ask me about them, which was a relief.

He was the pediatric infectious disease specialist and just hearing those words alone nearly sent me into hysterics. He did his best to calm me down, emphasizing that many more tests still needed to be done, but as of right now it was too soon to tell what was going on with my son.

For now, they were waiting for the blood test results, which they would have in a few hours. Once the blood tests were in, he would know which tests were needed next.

One step at a time. Detective work, really. Looking for clues, following up on hunches. Following the evidence.

Now I was alone with my son while he slept fitfully, looking so damn tiny in his bed. Just a small mound of dark hair and chubby red cheeks.

Hard as it was to do, I briefly left his side to go outside and make all the phone calls and text messages I needed to make. My sister assured me she would pick up my daughter. My ex-husband never called back. Neither did Kingsley.

Back in my son's room, I sat on the edge of his bed and held his left hand. The curtains were drawn and the lights were low. We had a room to ourselves, which was just as well, because I couldn't stop crying. The black halo that surrounded his body seemed to have grown a few millimeters as well. I didn't know much about the spirit world, but I was certain that I knew what I was seeing.

His soul was leaving.

Or perhaps it was already gone.

No, I thought. I refused to believe that.

He was just sick. Very sick. I am looking at the aura of a sick boy, that is all. A very sick boy. *My* sick boy.

Shit.

The light particles that flitted through the room, swirling and flashing and illuminating the air, disappeared completely into his aura. My hand, which glowed silverish to my own eyes, seemed to disappear into the blackness, as well. It was as if I had plunged my hand into freshly turned soil.

Graveyard soil.

I sat like that until the blood tests came back, miserable and borderline hysterical. The doctor returned and talked about normocytic anemia and thrombocytosis and blood count. He discussed something called an erythrocyte sedimentation rate and C-reactive protein levels being elevated. None of it sounded good to me. As he spoke, the doctor bit his lip a lot and looked grave and I sensed from him extreme concern and even alarm.

He next ordered liver function tests, an electrocardiogram, an echocardiogram, an ultrasound and a urinalysis.

And while they poked and prodded my son, my ex-husband Danny appeared in the doorway of the hospital room.

Chapter Twenty-four

He blinked, taking in the scene.

It was quite a scene. Three nurses and two doctors, all swarming around my son, who appeared to doze in and out of sleep. Or in and out of consciousness.

In our separation, Danny had proven to be particularly vindictive and mean-spirited. Unless, of course, you saw things from his point of view. Admittedly, very few people on the face of this earth would ever find themselves in his peculiar position. His once mostly happy household had been turned upside down. His wife of five years (which was how long we had been married prior to my attack) was suddenly not the person he had wed...and for the next six years Danny didn't handle things very well.

Yes, eleven years of marriage down the drain.

Would it have taken a special man to be strong

and stay by my side? Certainly. It also would have taken true love, too. That was, perhaps, the hardest realization of all. That my husband didn't love me enough to be there for me.

So, yes, if you saw things from his point of view then perhaps some of his actions began to make sense.

Some.

The cheating part was unforgivable. Call me what you want, but I didn't deserve that. Next, he had fought for sole custody of the children. He believed I could hurt them. That if I was desperate enough, or hungry enough, I might feed on my own children. Insanity, of course. If I was desperate enough or hungry enough, my neighbor's yipping chihuahua would suddenly go missing.

Fighting for the well-being of our children was admirable enough on Danny's part, although there was no basis for it. I had never once exhibited any lack of control. My children received nothing but love from me. I suspected he was doing it out of spite. To purposefully hurt me.

Danny wasn't a bad father. Sure, he worked too much and often missed out on anything that had to do with school and sports, but he made up for it the best way he could. Often he read to them at night. As I worked in my office, I would listen to him patiently explain the meanings of words and help his son and daughter pronounce them. Often I would hear little Anthony giggle at *Curious George* or Tammy beg him to read one more page of

Twilight. (Ironic, I know.) He spoke gently to each of them, sometimes so quietly that I never knew what he told them. I always wondered what they talked about, but I never wanted to ask. It seemed so personal. Just a son and a father, or a daughter and her father, exchanging sweet moments meant only for each other.

We'd gotten along like this for many years, living in quiet desperation, our kids content enough, but our marriage collapsing. I would have continued living like this forever. I was a monster and Danny seemed to at least accept me.

But it all came to a crashing end months ago when I had caught him cheating.

Danny still stood in the doorway, unsure what to do. His tie was still pushed up against his Adam's apple, and he looked pale and worried. He was still wearing his nice Italian suit. Danny rarely wore his nice suits, so he must have been in court today. An injury attorney, Danny hated going to court. Injury attorneys prefer to settle over the phone. They like easy, cut-and-dried cases. Anyway, if he had been in court, that might explain why he had been so short over the phone.

He finally spotted me in the far corner of the room, where I had sat while the doctors and nurses swarmed over my son. A few long strides later and he was sitting in the spare seat next to me, where he surprised the hell out of me by leaning over and giving me a small hug. I didn't hug him back.

"How is he, Sam?"

I started to tell him what I knew, but only about six coherent words came out. I broke down completely, sobbing hard into my hands, and I was slightly less surprised when Danny reached over again and pulled me into his shoulder.

Chapter Twenty-five

We were sitting side by side at the foot of my son's hospital bed. It was after hours, although "after hours" didn't mean much in a children's hospital intensive-care unit, since parents or guardians are usually permitted to stay with their children overnight.

We had been sitting there quietly for some time before I realized Danny had been holding my hand. I gently pulled it away, shocked and surprised all over again. Danny hadn't held my hand in six years. And if he did happen to touch me, it was always immediately followed by a visible shudder.

He wasn't shuddering now. Why, I don't know, and I certainly didn't care. Danny was the least of my concerns.

Anthony was breathing lightly on his own. Occasionally his aura would flash yellow, but mostly it was a deep black. Interestingly, bigger flashes of light seemed to hover over his body, and then scuttle away again like frightened fish. I sensed these could be other entities. But I wasn't sure. How could I be sure? I didn't know what the hell was going on with myself half the time.

Another curious glob of light came over him, hovering briefly over his head, and then seemed to dart around my son almost hectically.

No, not hectically.

Playfully.

It was the spirit of a child, I realized. And I was suddenly certain this child had died in this hospital. A ghost child. Trying to play with my son.

I took in a lot of air but the sound was strangled and Danny glanced sharply over at me. He didn't seem to know what to do with his hand now that I had removed mine from his.

"What?" he asked.

"Nothing," I said. I had long ago learned not to share my supernatural experiences with Danny. Such experiences served only to freak him out and distance him even further. Now, I just didn't care to share anything with him.

As I watched the amorphous light zigzag over my son's inert body, I thought of another child. A girl who was being held prisoner by God knows who. A girl who was alone and scared and probably hurt.

I looked at Danny. "Will you stay with Anthony?"

My ex-husband blinked, and then his eyes

narrowed. "Of course. Are you going somewhere?"

"Yes."

"I want to talk to you about something, Sam," he said, and I heard, amazingly, desperation and a hint of something else in his voice. What that hint was, I refused to believe.

"Can it wait?"

He almost reached out for my hand again, but stopped. I noticed a subtle ripple of revulsion pass through him, but he fought through it. "Yes, it can. When will you be back?"

I stood and grabbed my purse. I looked at my sleeping son. I looked at the impenetrable black halo that surrounded him. I decided against sharing any information with Danny, especially about the black halo. I also didn't want to talk about the phone call with little Maddie. Danny had lost his intimacy privilege long ago, and was nowhere near my inner circle.

I said, "I might be out all night."

He nodded. "It's okay. I'll be here. You have work to do. Anthony isn't going anywhere. Are you working a case?"

"Yes."

"An important case?"

"Very."

He nodded again. "I'll be here all night. I took half the day off tomorrow, too." He motioned to the nearby, partially open window which showed a sliver of silver-tipped clouds in the night sky. "Probably wouldn't be a good idea to have you sleeping here in the morning, right? Might raise a few suspicions."

I fought through my own shock and surprise of Danny showing an ounce of consideration. I said, "I'll try to make it back as soon as I can. Call me if anything comes up."

He nodded, and almost reached for me. I shrank back.

"Where are you going?" he asked.

"Out," I said, and left.

Chapter Twenty-six

McDonald's was hopping.

The smell of French fries hung heavy in the air. I hadn't eaten a French fry in over a half a decade. I wondered if they still tasted perfect. A creepy, life-sized, cardboard clown grinned at me from a far corner. Outside, shoeless children swarmed over the mother of all jungle gyms. A half-masticated chicken nugget sat under a nearby plastic booth.

And hanging from the ceiling above the counter was a video surveillance camera.

Bingo.

According to my Google map search, this was the closest McDonald's to Maddie's last known address—the same address where I had found the working meth lab and the not-so-working dead man.

I headed over to the counter, where a teenage Hispanic girl smiled at me blankly from behind a cash register. Instead of ordering, I asked to see the McManager.

***

Now I was sitting in the McDonald's manager's office. It wasn't much of an office. It was just a desk at one end of a narrow room. At the other end was the employee's time clock and the drive-thru window.

"We have to make this quick," he said. He was a very short, oddly shaped man with a bad limp. So bad, in fact, that I think his right leg might have been a prosthetic.

"Or the clown gets pissed," I said.

He grinned. "Something like that."

He didn't bother introducing himself. I guess when you're wearing name tags, introducing yourself is redundant. Anyway, according to his shiny black and silver tag, his name was Bill, and he was the general manager.

He listened to my story attentively. As he listened, he leaned a little to the right. He seemed to be mildly in pain. I would be, too, if I was sitting on half an ass. I concluded my story with my request to view the surveillance video.

"And you're working with the police?"

I gave him Detective Hanner's card. "Call her if you'd like."

He took it from me, studied it. "I'll do that. But I'll have to get approval from my district manager before I release the surveillance video."

"Of course."

"It's not that I don't want to help you."

"I understand."

"We just have procedure."

"Of course you do."

"Aw, fuck it. There's a missing girl. Hang on, and I'll get you set up in here. I'm not exactly sure how to run some of these electronic gizmos, though."

"I'm pretty handy with electronic gizmos."

"Of course you are. A regular James Bond."

"Minus the babes and the goofy accent."

He grinned again. "Hang on."

He got up and limped out of the office. As I waited for him to return, I thought of my son and the black aura, and a crushing despair unlike anything I had ever felt took hold of me right there. All thought escaped me. Rational thought, that is. I had an image of myself grabbing him and jumping through the hospital window. Of me running off into the night with my son in my arms. Where I would go, I didn't know, but I had an image of us together, somewhere, alone, while I willed him to perfect health. The image was strong. The image was real, and I wondered if it was perhaps precognitive.

Could I now see into the future?

I didn't know, but more than likely it was just an image of a helpless mother doing something, anything, to help her sick son.

Bill came back with a remote control and a small three-ring binder. He sat back at his desk, easing himself down slowly. As he did so, gasping and wincing, a wrecked motorcycle briefly flashed before me. I saw it steaming and twisted on the asphalt.

"You were in a motorcycle accident," I said suddenly and without thinking.

Bill snapped his head up. He had been flipping through the binder. Now his hand paused in mid-flip. His eyes narrowed. "How did you know?"

I could have pointed to the Harley-Davidson picture frame or the Harley-Davidson coffee mug, both of which were sitting on his desk. I could have told him that it had been a lucky conjecture. But I didn't. I was too mentally exhausted for lies and half-truths.

"I had a vision of you crashing. I saw the twisted wreck of your bike. I saw the twisted wreck of your leg."

He continued looking at me, and then finally nodded. "Yeah, I crashed it. Took a right turn too wide. Head on into a minivan. To this day I have no clue why I'm alive."

"You still ride, though," I said.

He nodded. "It's the only thing that keeps me sane. How did you know?"

"Lucky guess."

"You're a freaky lady."

"You have no idea."

"And this little girl," he said.

"She was here." I said. "I know it."

"There's a lot of tape here. I was just looking through the instructions on how to—"

"Video surveillance 101," I said. "I can manage."

He pushed the folder over to me. "Here's the passwords to access the program. It's all stored on remote hard drives, but we can access it from here, and elsewhere, too. We have a lot of shit that goes down in our parking lots. Cops are always here checking out our video feeds."

"Thank you," I said. "I'll be fine."

"Do you know what day she was here?"

"No clue."

"Do you know what the girl looks like?"

"No clue."

"Do you know what the bad guys look like?"

"I have an idea," I said, thinking of the big black man in Maddie's memory. "I do have a picture of the mother."

"It's a start," he said.

The strong smell of French fries seemed to eddy in his back office. I said, "You ever get sick of the smell of French fries?"

"Honestly?" he said. "It turns my stomach."

Chapter Twenty-seven

The surveillance program was one I was familiar with. The images recorded were stored on a Cisco Video Surveillance Storage System, which permitted the authorized user, yours truly, to access any point in time over the past five years.

So where to begin? Admittedly, using my apparently increasing psychic powers could help here, but I wasn't sure how to harness such extrasensory perceptions to an actual date. Maybe someday I would get to the point where if I sat quietly enough, an actual date would just appear in my thoughts. I wasn't quite there yet, and I somehow doubted my gifts could be *that* accurate.

So I went about this as any investigator would. Deduction, deduction, deduction.

According to official accounts, Madison and her mother had gone missing about three months ago. According to Bill, the "My Little Pony" Happy

Meal theme had concluded nearly four months ago. Those timelines nearly coincided.

I removed the police file from my handbag, opened it, and looked again at the only picture of Maddie's mother on record. The woman was probably twenty-two but she looked fifty. She also looked like a typical user: skeletal, pallid, lost. Meth eats away at the brain like a tapeworm from undercooked pork, and the results are typically the same: extreme paranoia, loss of motor control, and a disinterest in anything that isn't meth. Even your kids. The woman in the picture—a mug shot taken of her years before—wouldn't have cared about her daughter's health. Or anyone's health. She cared only for getting high and it had gotten her killed. And put her daughter in harm's way.

I decided I would start four months ago and work my way forward.

And that's exactly what I did for the next five hours. Going through day after day, studying the faces of anyone who was towing a child with them. The camera was a good one, and it was set up behind the counter, looking over the employee's shoulder. There were only three active cash registers and the wide-lensed camera was able to capture the faces of any and everyone who walked up to the counter. Little kids tended to disappear *below* the counter, but I generally had a good view of any kids approaching the registers. Not that it mattered since I had no clue what Maddie looked like anyway.

I'll know her when I see her, I thought. Or so I hoped.

As I went through the days and fast-forwarding only to promising targets, I thought about my son, Danny, Fang and Kingsley.

The men in my life.

My thoughts lingered on Kingsley and something pulled at me. Something important. What was it? I wasn't sure. Something he had said perhaps. Something that had been important, or could be important. Whatever it was, it got my heart racing.

I would think about it later, whatever it was.

Days and weeks passed. I paused often and studied faces. There were a few possibilities that made me sit up and take notice. But upon further view, the woman/child or man/child didn't add up. The girl was too perky. The mother was too happy. The father seemed particularly loving. None of this added up, at least not to me.

I continued forward. Hours sped by. Whole families appeared in the frame. I wasn't looking for whole families. I was looking for a lonely girl and someone else. Someone that made sense.

And then I found them.

The girl was dirty, dressed in a stained dress that had a torn Strawberry Shortcake patch over her chest. She trailed behind a woman who seemed confused by the McDonald's order board. Who gets confused over a McDonald's order board? It's the most famous menu in the world. She frowned and bit her lip and seemed to talk to herself. The woman herself was dressed in torn denim shorts. One leg was torn higher than the other. A white pocket hung free, squared off with a package of cigarettes. Not once did the mother look back for her little girl, who stayed behind her, swaying gently to unheard music. The girl hooked one of her tiny fingers in her mouth and waited for her mother. She could have just turned and walked out of the restaurant and her mother would never know, and perhaps never care. The little girl kept swaying. She was barefoot. Her feet were dirty. So were her ankles. The mother had been wearing flip flops, but now I couldn't see the mother's feet, since they were below the counter. The girl was far back, easily in the camera frame. I stared at the girl, fascinated, my eyes glued to the monitor in front of me. In my thoughts, I could hear the girl talking. *This* little girl.

"He kilt my mother. He shot her dead."

"Maddie," I whispered.

And as the mother fumbled her way through the order, the worker placed an open Happy Meal on the counter, and as Lauren dug into her pocket, presumably for money, someone else came into the McDonald's. A man. A big black man wearing a long trenchcoat. Maddie saw him and shrank away immediately. The man said something sharply and the mother nodded. She, too, shrank away.

The man jerked his head and little Maddie followed him deeper into McDonald's, where she disappeared out of the camera frame.

I watched Lauren count out her money, then wait for her change, and finally hurry deeper into the restaurant. Thirty-three minutes later, the happy family left together, with Maddie trailing behind, forgotten, her finger hooked in her mouth.

Holding her Happy Meal box.

Chapter Twenty-eight

The surveillance software has a nice feature that allows you to freeze a face and zero in on it, which I did for Maddie, her mother, and the man.

Now I was sitting outside a Starbucks on a cool night with Detective Hanner of the Fullerton Police Missing Persons Unit. Neither of us was drinking a coffee, which was a damn shame. Detective Hanner was studying the photos and making small, disapproving noises. I wondered if she knew she was making those sounds. Then again, my hearing tends to be exceptional these days, so perhaps I was never meant to hear her small, disapproving noises.

She looked up from the pictures.

"Good work," she said.

"I sometimes get it right."

"Detective Sherbet said that if anyone was likely to turn something up, it would be you."

"Detective Sherbet says the nicest things."

Hanner shook her head. "Actually, rarely. He likes you."

"The feeling is mutual."

She tapped the photo of the black man in a trench coat. Her fingernail was long. And sharp. I might have gasped a little. "He was with them around the time of their disappearance," Hanner said. "He's a person of interest."

"He's got my interest," I said.

"This photo will be everywhere as soon as I get back to the station. We'll catch this bastard."

"If you don't mind, I would still like to help."

"Hey, Maddie picked you. Maybe there's something bigger at work here. Of course I want your help. After I drop by the station, I'm heading out to work three more missing person cases. One of them is an old lady from a nearby nursing home. My second call about her in two weeks. Found her last time partying with some local crackheads, high as a kite, dancing the Charleston naked."

I snorted. "Now that's getting high old school."

"If you saw the place she lived, you probably wouldn't blame her. Creepy as hell. An old folks home for retired witches and wizards, if you ask me. A sort of Hogwarts for old farts."

"Here in this city?" I asked.

She looked at me for a heartbeat or two before smiling. "You would be surprised what's in this city."

I found her oddly closed off, as if there some sort of shield around her. Her aura, I noticed, was an even blue. The same color as Kingsley's. It also hovered only a few inches from her skin, same as with Kingsley.

"I like you," she added. "We should get a drink some time, and talk." She winked, and as she did so, her pupils shrank noticeably. "You know...girl talk."

"Sure," I said.

"Good." She got up and threw her handbag over one shoulder. She reached out for my hand. "Let me know what you find, and thanks again."

As always, I hesitated before shaking any hand. But hers I was almost eager to shake. I did so now, taking her small hand in my own, and I was not very surprised to discover it was ice cold.

She stared at me intently, just a few feet away. The hair at the back of my neck was standing on end. And then she winked at me, turned, and strode off through the parking lot.

She moved gracefully and effortlessly, and I watched her until she got into her dark Mercury Sable and drove out of the parking lot, and as she did so, I was certain I had just met my first vampire.

Chapter Twenty-nine

I sent Danny a text asking for an update, and he responded almost instantly: Anthony was in stable condition and sleeping soundly. I texted Danny back and reminded him that his cell phone was supposed to be turned off.

He wrote back: *Yes, Mommy.* And added a happy face.

Danny was being oddly playful and, well, *nice.* Maybe it had to do with his son being seriously ill. I didn't know, but I found it creepy as hell. Any feelings I had had for Danny were long gone.

And what did he want to talk about? I didn't know.

I sat in my minivan for a few minutes, wondering what I should do next. The museum could wait. The girl needed my help, except I didn't have much to go on. I removed my copy of the picture of the big black man, and I suddenly knew what I needed most.

Manpower.

***

His business card was still in the van's center console. I turned the interior light on, even though I really didn't need it.

His card was simple but compelling. On the right side were written the words: Jim Knighthorse, Private Investigator. On the other side, filling the entire left half of the card, was his picture. He was smiling. A sort of crooked half-smile that showed a lot of teeth. The smile was arrogant. The smile was casual. The light in his eyes was filled with good humor, as if he alone was in on a joke.

I had met the tall man a few weeks earlier. At the time, he had radiated a quiet strength and a lot of cockiness. Both were good qualities when it came to investigations. In fact, I would argue that both were *ideal* in a good investigator. But more than anything, I had sensed a sort of old-school chivalry in him, that he was a man who protected those who couldn't protect themselves.

I needed this man.

I made the call and, despite the fact that I sensed I had interrupted him from something important, he immediately agreed to meet me.

***

"I had a strange feeling we would meet again," he said, as he approached my van.

Correction: *swaggered* to my van. Even though he limped noticeably.

"Maybe you're psychic," I said.

"I'm a lot of things," he said, grinning easily, "but being psychic isn't one of them."

By a *lot of things*, I knew he meant *a lot of good things*. I shook my head. The guy was too much. But he was hard not to love.

I was standing outside my minivan, itself parked outside a Norm's in Santa Ana. When you work the night shift like me, you're fully aware of each and every all-night restaurant, even if, like me, you can't actually partake from them, outside of water and cheap wine.

Knighthorse glanced over at the dimly lit Norms. "You would make a cheap date."

"What can I say, I'm a simple woman."

He glanced at me sideways. "I somehow doubt that. Anyone who hangs out with Orange County's most famous defense attorney has a few surprises up her sleeve."

He was, of course, talking about Kingsley, whom I was with when I first met Knighthorse on the beach a few weeks ago. "Okay, maybe one or two," I said.

He folded his arms over his chest and leaned a hip against the van's front fender. Although it was chilly out, he was wearing only a black tee shirt and blue jeans.

I'm a woman. I'm recently divorced. Outside of an orgasm a few weeks ago, I hadn't had any sex in six years. The orgasm, I think, opened the floodgates.

So I'll admit it. I found myself staring at his biceps. Just his biceps, I swear. The way they reflected the yellowish parking lot lights. The way the thick veins protruded nearly an inch off his muscles. The way the muscle itself seemed to undulate even with the slightest of movements. I have keen eyesight, and I used every bit of it as I studied his biceps.

He looked down at his shirt. "Is there something on me? It's jelly, isn't it? I just ate a jelly donut and I felt some of it drop, I just didn't know where."

"It's not jelly. Sorry, I just have a lot on my mind."

He quit inspecting his shirt and went back to leaning a hip against my fender.

"So tell me more about the little girl."

I did, recalling everything I could. I handed him a photocopy of the trio at McDonald's. He studied it closely. Holding it up to the parking lot lights. Myself, I could see it perfectly, but he didn't need to know that.

"We'll need to canvass the area," he said.

"That's what I figured."

"A guy like this, some lowlife drug-dealing asshole, is probably on the move, especially if he just killed the mother."

"We're making a lot of leaps here," I said. "The guy could be innocent. Maybe he's an old friend."

Knighthorse shook his head and came over to me. He smelled of raspberry donuts and Old Spice. God, I loved a man who wore Old Spice. The jelly donuts, not so much. He held up the picture of the black man and pointed.

"Look here," he said. "He's wearing a trench coat for a reason."

"Covering a gun?"

"Why else? It's 80 degrees here 300 days of the year. But look..." Knighthorse shuffled through the three photos I had given him. "There. Look."

I saw it. It was a slight bulge at the man's hip. "A gun," I said.

"Of course."

"And we're not racially stereotyping him?" I said. "Because he's black?"

Knighthorse looked down at me, and all the swagger and cockiness was gone, and I saw the real investigator in him, the man who took his job deadly serious. "What does your gut say about him?"

"That he's our guy. That he killed Maddie's mom, or at least knows the person who did. That he presently has Maddie somewhere, perhaps hurting her, perhaps killing her."

Knighthorse's jaw rippled. I think his teeth actually ground together. "Yeah, that's what my gut says, too. And race has nothing to do with that."

"What are the chances he's a drug dealer?"

"About the same chance that I'm tall and roguishly good-looking."

I shook my head. The guy was too much. I said, "So, if he supplies drugs to the neighborhood...."

"Few will talk," he said.

"That, and they're probably scared of him."

"Someone will talk," said Knighthorse.

"And if he did kill Maddie's mother, then he's laying low."

Knighthorse winked. "We're gonna need more manpower."

Chapter Thirty

There were four of us now.

We were all sitting in the McDonald's in Buena Park, the same McDonald's where, for all I knew, Maddie's mother was last seen alive.

I was drinking a cup of water. Knighthorse had just polished off three Big Macs and a large vanilla shake. Now he was munching on a bag of fries the size of my purse. The fries smelled so damn good that I nearly reached over for one. I resisted. Fries and my undead stomach do not mix.

The thirty-something man sitting next to Knighthorse was about a foot shorter. He was also a specialist in finding the missing, particularly children. His name was Spinoza, and he was a private investigator out of Los Angeles and a friend of Knighthorse. Spinoza, who was oddly shy for a private eye, was shrouded in a heavy layer of darkness. His aura itself seemed weighed down by something.

Guilt, I suddenly thought. *Something is eating away at him. Tearing him apart.* And just as I thought that, a brief image appeared in my thoughts, so horrific and heartbreaking that I nearly broke down myself. It was snapshot of him holding a burned body. A tiny burned body.

It was his son, and now I understood the waves of guilt.

The image was of a car accident. Like with the McDonald's manager, I saw a burned-out vehicle, but this time I received another sensory hit: The smell of alcohol, along with the smell of burned flesh.

Sweet Jesus.

His palpable waves of guilt nearly overwhelmed me in my current, fragile state, and I was beginning to see the downside of this ESP business.

I need to learn how to shut this shit off, I thought.

Spinoza was friendly enough and had smiled and shaken my hand, but he easily lapsed into a dark silence that made it nearly impossible to warm up to the man.

Sitting next to him was another investigator— yet another specialist in finding the missing. His name was Aaron King and he was older than the hills. He was also damn good-looking and frustratingly familiar-looking.

And the psychic hit I got from him was an unusual one: *Mr. Aaron King had a secret. A big secret.*

He caught me looking at him and gave me a beautiful smile, complete with twinkling eyes. I found my heart beating a little faster.

Aaron King and Spinoza (I never did catch his first name) passed on eating and instead sipped from oversized drinks. Men and their oversized drinks. Sheesh. They examined the photos while I recounted the events of the last few days, beginning with the first phone call from Maddie, my discussion with Chad, my conversation with Detective Hanner, Maddie's second call, the meth lab and dead body, the Happy Meal, and the video surveillance.

"All this from a wrong number," said Aaron. God, I loved the lilt to his voice. A hint of an accent. Melodious. A beautiful and agonizingly familiar voice.

"Probably not a wrong number," said Spinoza. The man spoke as if it were a great effort. As if it took all his energy and strength to form the words. If ever there was a man who needed a hug, it was him.

Knighthorse nodded. "Your number was programmed into the phone. No way a kid that young finds you in the phone book."

"Could be our guy's phone," said Spinoza.

Knighthorse looked at me. "Any reason why a six foot five black thug would have your number programmed in his phone?"

"Maybe he's looking for a good time?" I said.

Knighthorse grinned, and so did Spinoza. I think. Aaron King chuckled lightly.

"Maybe it wasn't his phone," offered Spinoza.

"Her mother's?" said King.

I nodded. "Maybe her mother gave it to her before her death."

Spinoza said, "Maybe she suspected something bad might happen. If so, she wanted her daughter to have it in case of an emergency."

"And she pre-programmed it with Samantha's info?" said Aaron King. "Why not the police?"

"Or maybe she took it off her mother's dead body," said Knighthorse, and the expression that briefly crossed his face was one of profound pain. Knighthorse, I realized, knew something about dead mothers. His own dead mother.

Jesus, we're all a mess, I thought.

"And you don't recognize the woman?" King asked me.

"No. And her name doesn't show up in any of my case files."

"Did you check all your case files?" asked King.

"All my files are in a database."

Knighthorse and King whistled. "Maybe I should get me one of those," said the old guy, winking at me in such a way that my stomach literally did a somersault.

Spinoza plowed forward. "Still, that doesn't

mean the mother, what's her name—"

"Lauren," I said.

"That doesn't mean Lauren didn't look you up prior to being killed. Maybe she knew something was wrong."

"Or something was about to go wrong," said King.

"Right," said Knighthorse. "She looks you up in the Yellow Pages, punches you in her phone for a later call."

"But never makes the call," I said.

"Right."

"Maybe the mother tried calling you, Samantha," said Spinoza. "Perhaps you were her last call."

"Except you were too damn busy with your database to pick up," said King. He winked at me, and I elbowed the old guy in the ribs. He chuckled again.

"If so," said Knighthorse, "then perhaps you were the last call she ever made. And if the call came through as blocked, which can be done automatically, then you would have no record of the call."

"It's a theory," I said.

Knighthorse said, "And then all the daughter had to do was hit redial."

"And she would call me," I said.

"Bingo."

We let that theory digest for a few seconds. Then Spinoza set his oversized drink down. No doubt his normal-sized bladder was bursting at the seams. "So let's hit it," he said.

And we did. But first he went to the bathroom.

Chapter Thirty-one

Private investigators seem to hold a certain allure for many people. I get that. TV has certainly made the work appear glamorous; after all, there's something exciting about being a lone wolf (no pun intended), working when you want, living on the edge of society, and catching the bad guys. The adventure. The excitement. The mystery.

Sorry folks, but fifty percent of P.I. work is following cheating spouses and doing background checks. And even then, the background work is getting sparser and sparser, thanks to so many new internet sites that do the work for us.

But, yeah, every now and then we do get a juicy case. And it can be fun. Especially when you do help those in need.

More often than not, P.I. work takes great patience, especially when you're watching a subject at home for days on end. Or when you're beating down doors looking for leads.

Like we were doing now.

Canvassing a targeted area will eventually turn up something. With enough people pounding doors and stopping people on the streets, someone, somewhere will recognize the man in the picture.

Canvassing is painstaking and frustrating at best, hopeless and infuriating at worst. And just when you think you couldn't knock on another door, or stop another stranger on the street, someone starts talking, and that someone will tell you exactly what you need to know.

Ideally.

So the four of us hit the pavement and, using a street map, centered our efforts on four different quadrants surrounding the meth house. I had the northeast section, which included a lot of rundown apartments, rundown homes, and a handful of motels. The guys didn't like me running off on my own but I reminded them that I was a highly trained federal agent. They didn't like it, and made me promise to keep my cell phone and pepper spray handy. I didn't have any pepper spray, but the old man Aaron gave me his.

I checked with Danny once, confirmed that Anthony was still sleeping, checked with my sister, confirmed Tammy was safe and sound at their home, and then hit the pavement.

And hit it hard.

***

We did this for four hours.

I questioned dozens and dozens, if not hundreds of people. I sensed that many of the young men recognized the man in the picture. None of them were talking. I would make them talk if I had to. I remembered where all of them lived.

Sometimes I don't play by the rules. Sometimes I make up the rules. Someone was going to talk, whether they wanted to or not.

A few of these men let it be known that they didn't appreciate me walking around and asking a lot of questions. One of these men might have threatened me. One of these men might have soon thereafter suffered a broken finger.

Might have.

I handed out all the fliers I had, each one with my cell phone number on the bottom and a promise that the call would remain confidential. And at the end of the night, with no one talking and the neighborhood shutting down, the four of us reconvened at the McDonald's. We discussed our options. We all felt we had hit the area pretty hard. Most of us felt someone knew something but wasn't talking. We all agreed that unless someone started talking soon, we would have to take drastic measures. None of us talked about what those drastic measures were. I suspected each of us had our own definitions.

Knighthorse and Spinoza would both be back tomorrow morning. I would be back in the evening. Aaron King had a lead or two he wanted to follow up tonight. He insisted on following up alone, stating he would use his old Southern charm to get the information he needed. He even winked. Hell, I was charmed ten times over.

As I stepped into my minivan, Knighthorse pulled up beside me in his classic Mustang. He cranked down his window and said he'd heard from someone on the street that a mean, dark-haired lady had broken some gangbanger's finger. His eyes narrowed. "That wouldn't have been you, would it?" he asked.

"Everything but the mean part. It's not nice to threaten a lady."

He threw back his head and laughed. "I knew you were a badass."

"Badder than most."

"Hey, that's my line," he said, winking. He rolled up his window and peeled out of the parking lot.

Spinoza followed behind in his nondescript Toyota Camry, a car much better suited for investigations than Knighthorse's eye-catching classic Mustang. He nodded at me and told me we would find her. I thanked the deeply troubled man for his help, and secretly hoped he would find himself.

As I started up my minivan—a vehicle even better suited for long surveillances—Aaron King sidled up to the window. His eyes twinkled. As if he was in on a private joke. Or if he knew a secret. I rolled down my window.

"We'll find that girl," he said. "I have a daughter. I can't stand the thought of a little girl alone and scared and possibly abused."

"I have a daughter, too," I said. "And a son."

But that was all I could get out. My voice caught in my throat.

Aaron King angled his beautiful face down into my window. "Is there something wrong, lil' darling?" he asked.

"No, I—" But my voice did it again. Or, rather, my throat did. It shut tight, and all I could do was shake my head.

But there was something so tender, so serene, so warm about Aaron King. I felt myself opening up to him, responding to him. Connecting with him.

I tried again. "My son..." But, dammit, that was all I could say. Even those words came out in a strangled choke.

Aaron reached through the driver's side window and gently touched my chin. "Hey, even highly trained federal agents cry," he said.

And I did. Hard. Much harder than I thought I would around a stranger. Aaron King let me cry. The hand he used to touch my cheek now reached around and patted my head and shoulders gently. He was a loving grandfather. A man with a big, beautiful heart.

And when I was all cried out, he rested his forehead against the upper window frame. "I'm sorry you're sad, lil' lady. But everything's going to be alright."

Some of the McDonald's yellowish parking lot light caught his eyes, and when he smiled again—a smile that was so bright that it lifted my spirits immediately—I got the mother of all psychic hits. So powerful...and so mind blowing. So much so that I was certain I had made it up.

No way, I thought.

But the hit persisted. His name wasn't Aaron King. At least, not the name the world knew him by.

Unbelievable.

"I'll call you tomorrow, Samantha Moon. And you can tell me about your son then."

I nodded, too dumbfounded to speak.

He winked at me. "Go take care of your son." And then he reached through the window and gave my chin a small boxing jab, smiled at me again, and walked back to his own car.

A Cadillac.

Might as well have been a *pink* Cadillac.

Chapter Thirty-two

Still reeling from my encounter with Aaron King, whose real name, of course, *wasn't* Aaron King, I found myself at the Wharton Museum.

Danny had promised to call me immediately if anything came up, and since I hadn't received a call, I might as well keep working, right? And with Aaron still working the case in Buena Park, I thought it was best to tackle some of my paying work.

I might be undead. I might drink blood. And I might be one hell of a freaky chick, but I still needed to feed my kids and pay my bills.

Still in my van, I removed my secret stash of foundation make-up, which I often applied heavily to my face and the back of my hands. I may not show up in mirrors or on surveillance video—weird as hell, I know—but the make-up still did. And after a long night of pounding doors and breaking fingers, well, I wasn't sure how much of my make-up was still in place.

I had already been introduced to the head night security guard, whose name was Eddie. Eddie was a heavy-set Hispanic guy who seemed as cool as cool gets, and oozed a smooth confidence. The way he carried himself, you would have thought he looked a little more like George Clooney and a lot less like Chris Farley.

Then again, I always did think Chris Farley was a cutie.

We were in Eddie's office, which was just inside the main doors of the museum. His office looked a little like Mission Control, minus all the nerds in white short-sleeved, button-down dress shirts. There were ten monitors placed in and around his desk, all providing live feeds from within the museum. While we sat, he cycled through some exterior cameras and some back-room cameras. All in all, there were over twenty cameras situated throughout the small museum.

Eddie leaned back in his swivel chair, a chair that looked abused and ready to give out. I was sitting in a metal foldout chair he had grabbed from a storage closet behind him. The cold metal was almost as cold as my own flesh.

Eddie, to his credit, rarely took his eyes off the monitors. There was a Starbucks coffee sitting next to a keyboard. The keyboard had old coffee stains on it. I wondered how many keyboards Eddie had fried spilling his coffees.

"Would you mind telling me about the night the crystal sculpture was stolen?" I asked.

He shrugged defensively. "Like any other night."

I waited. Eddie stared at the monitors. Apparently that's all I was getting.

I said, "So nothing out of the ordinary?"

"Nothing other than our back-room cameras suddenly stopped working."

"Did the theft take place in the back room?"

"Wow, you're good," he said, still not looking at me. "It's no wonder they hired you."

I ignored the remark. "How long were the cameras not working?"

"Twenty-one minutes."

"Did you catch this immediately?"

He shook his head. "Both pictures were frozen in place. How they did it, we have no clue. But the image looked fine, until I noticed the timer had stopped."

"And how long until you noticed that?"

"Thirty, forty minutes."

"Long enough for the egg to be stolen."

"Yes."

"Could have happened to anyone," I said.

He squinted at me, trying to decide if I was being as big of an asshole as he was, and finally decided that I wasn't. He relaxed a little. "I guess so, yes."

"Where in the back room did the theft occur?"

He pointed to one of the images on the screen.

"There. The shipping and receiving room. We had just received the collection from the artist himself."

"And does the artist know of the theft?"

"Not yet, as far as I'm aware."

"When is the exhibit set to debut?"

"One week."

"And the cameras caught nothing?"

"Not a thing."

"Was anything else stolen?"

"Just the crystal egg."

I knew the museum had insurance to cover such a loss, but there was no insurance to cover one's reputation. From what I understood, the theft would be a black eye that the museum could ill afford.

I said, "Other than security guards, does anyone else work the night shift?"

"No, although sometimes the docents and museum staff put in late hours, especially when a new exhibit is about to open."

"Were any of the museum staff working the night the sculpture was stolen?"

"Yes, but they had left hours before."

"How many security guards typically work the night shift?"

"We have four working after hours. Ten when the museum is open. We only have three working tonight."

"Why's that?"

Now Eddie looked pissed. "No clue. Thad never showed."

"What's Thad's full name?"

"Thad Perry."

"Was Thad working on the night in question?"

"No."

"Has he ever not shown up before?"

"Never."

"So you would call this unusual behavior?"

"Extremely."

"May I have a list of the names and numbers to all four security guards working that night?"

Eddie nodded once and slowly eased forward. He tapped a few keys at his keyboard, somehow avoiding knocking his coffee over in the process. This time. He wrote down four names and four phone numbers on a mini-sized pad of legal paper. He handed me the paper. His name was on the list.

"At the time of the theft, where were you?"

Eddie looked at me long and hard. I wasn't getting a guilty hit from Eddie. But I was getting a hostile one. He said, "I was here, manning the desk."

"The whole night?"

"Yes," he said, "the whole night."

"What about bathroom breaks?"

He jabbed a thumb behind him toward the small storage room. A storage room that, I saw, doubled as a small bathroom. "I take my potty breaks in there."

"Who on this list is working tonight?"

"Just Joey."

"I'd like to talk to Joey."

"Of course."

"Were any other private investigators hired to work the case?" I asked.

He nodded. "You and two other private dicks."

He grinned and flicked his gaze toward my crotch. He enjoyed being crude in my presence. I wondered if he would enjoy being dropped into a Jacuzzi from a fourth story balcony.

Crudeness aside, it made sense to hire more than one detective. People did it all the time. When a customer found a human finger in a bowl of Wendy's chili, Wendy's hired over ten private eyes to break the case, which one of them finally did. The finger belonged to one of the customer's friends, a finger he had lost in an industrial accident. The friends then cooked up a scheme, no pun intended, and it might have worked if not for the tenacity of one detective, and the foresight of Wendy's to hire a slew of them.

"Has anyone made any headway?" I asked.

He flicked his gaze at me sideways. Cool as cool gets. "The egg is still missing if that answers your question."

"Oh, most definitely. I'd like to see the back room now."

He reached inside his desk and handed me a generic security badge. "It's a temporary badge. Swipe it, then key in '0000'. And I'll send Joey over, too."

He showed me on the monitors where to find the back room. I thanked him for his time. Eddie nodded once.

Too cool to nod twice.

Chapter Thirty-three

I could almost feel Eddie watching me as I worked my way through the museum, past exhibits called Native American Art and Ancient Art of China. I wondered what my butt looked like on camera. Probably cute. Maybe a little bubbly, since my daughter called me bubble butt sometimes.

I made my way through the Spirits and Headhunters collections, stopping briefly to ogle at a half dozen shrunken heads.

Real, honest-to-God shrunken heads.

And they call me a monster.

I moved through another room, and entered the Mayan exhibit, complete with a stone sarcophagus and beautifully adorned stelae covered in hieroglyphs. The room was particularly alive with zigzagging light...and much bigger balls of light. I knew now what these bigger balls of light were.

Spirits.

The balls seemed to orient on me. Sometimes they grew bigger and sometimes smaller. Sometimes they hovered just above the floor or shot up to the far corners of the room. One or two of them followed behind me.

They were silent, almost curious.

But they could see me. I felt it. I sensed it. Eyes were on me. Unseen eyes. And it wasn't Eddie ogling me from the Command Center.

And if the ghosts could see me, what else could they see?

Perhaps a crime?

I thought about that as I found the back door. I swiped the security card and entered the cryptic "0000" code and found myself in a spacious room. Spacious and dark.

I was about to flip on a light switch when one of the balls of light that had been following me slipped under the closed door and hovered before me.

I was standing off to the side of the door, partially facing a vast room with shelves and storage everywhere. I knew that most museums only displayed a small fraction of their exhibits, and that most pieces were in special storage within the museum, usually in basements. The Wharton, it appeared, didn't have a basement, and allotted this vast room for storage.

The room was pitch black, but that didn't stop me from seeing deep within it, and what I could see were various glass-walled bays that were probably temperature controlled. The bays contained what appeared to be rolling racks of paintings. No doubt very expensive paintings.

The ball of light crackled with energy. Yes, I could almost hear it now, a steady hum, too low for most people to hear. The hair on my arms was standing on end and I realized that the ball of light was trying to draw energy from me.

So how much energy did an ice-cold vampire have?

I didn't know, but the ball of light began taking on shape and as it did so, my mouth dropped open. And the more it took on shape, the more my mouth dropped open.

It seemed to pull in the surrounding particles of light, gathering them together the way cotton candy collects around a twirling stick.

The particles of light blended with the ball of light, which began to take on shape. A human shape. And when my mouth had dropped fully open, the vague figure of a tall, thin man stood fully before me.

And, if I wasn't mistaken, he bowed slightly.

Chapter Thirty-four

I almost bowed back, but stopped myself.

The hair along my arms was standing on end, and I saw why. A part of his crackling, frenetic, human-like essence had reached out to me. It reminded me of a white blood cell attacking a virus. I wasn't sure what was happening, until it hit me: he was drawing energy from me.

Amazing.

He wasn't a composed whole. A few times some of the light energy that composed his body seemed to disperse and scatter like frightened fish, only to reform again into the tall, thin man standing before me.

The entity tilted his head slightly to one side, and as he did so, a brief image flashed into my thoughts. The image was of a kindly old man and his wife. They were standing in front of a small building, smiling happily. I had, of course, seen pictures of this same building, especially during the past few days. It was the original 7,000 square foot site of the Wharton Museum. In the picture, was the same old couple, smiling happily.

The Whartons.

Next, a single word appeared in my thoughts. Honestly, I didn't know if I thought it or heard it. Either way, it appeared just inside my eardrum:

"Come."

***

With that, the entity that I now thought of as Mr. Wharton drifted away. As he drifted away, he lost some of his shape and looked, more than anything, like a floating, glowing amoeba.

He wanted me to follow him. That much I was certain of.

I obliged, following the amorphous ball of energy deeper into the back room, past rows and shelves of Native American art, African art and Chinese art. In fact, dozens and dozens of rows. The majority of the shelves were filled with wooden and clay sculptures, weapons that still looked like they could seriously do some harm, and what had to be priceless jewelry. The jewelry was behind glass cases, as were some of the more delicate pieces. Not surprisingly, Mr. Wharton seemed to know his way.

We passed the small shipping and receiving room, which was lined with metal tables and boxes of all shapes and sizes. Some looked like they were going, and no doubt some still needed to be received. What were in those boxes was anyone's guess.

He led me deeper. Or, rather, the glowing ball of light led me deeper, as it had now lost all human shape. It was dimmer back here, and there was only a single security camera a few rows down. Eddie would have a hard time seeing me. No doubt he was wondering what the hell I was doing back here. I was wondering, too.

Mr. Wharton hung a left. And by hanging a left, I mean the ball of light that was the ghostly imprint of Mr. Wharton, went *through* some shelves and entered a side corridor. I hung the left the old-fashioned way.

He continued on, and so did I.

The camera, I saw, did not reach down this side corridor, which meant that Mr. Wharton and I were alone. And at the far end of the corridor was a massive storage freezer that looked vaguely like a coffin.

I wasn't sure what the museum would need such a storage freezer for, until I remembered the shrunken heads outside. No doubt the museum kept anything biological in cold storage. At least, that's what I would do if I had a collection of shrunken heads.

Crackling and spitting energy and doing his best impression of a human torch, Mr. Wharton materialized again. He stood next to the freezer.

As I approached, Mr. Wharton actually stepped

aside to give me access.

Ghostly etiquette. Nice.

I reached down and slowly opened the lid. Cool air rushed out, and the stench of frozen meat. And when the swirling mist had subsided, a very dead face was looking up at me from the depths of the freezer. Wearing a museum guard uniform. I think I had just found Thad, the missing guard.

Two dead bodies in two days.

I was on a roll.

Chapter Thirty-five

It was late, and I was sitting in Kingsley's spacious living room. I had spent the last few hours talking to various Santa Ana homicide detectives. When they were done asking questions and satisfied with my answers, I texted Kingsley and he invited me over.

Franklin, Kingsley's butler, was noisily preparing our drinks in the kitchen. The kitchen was down the hall and around a corner and through a swinging door. Something banged loudly, or possibly even broke.

"I think Franklin is letting it be known that he doesn't appreciate my late-night sojourns," I said.

"Luckily, Franklin doesn't have much say in the matter," said Kingsley. "How's your son doing?"

"Not good."

"I'm sorry, Sam."

I nodded and fought through the tears. It was amazing how quickly tears came these days.

The big defense attorney, who had been lounging in a chair-and-a-half across from me, sat forward. The chair-and-a-half was barely big enough to contain him. Kingsley, I could tell, wanted to reach out for me, but stopped himself. Our relationship had cooled noticeably a few weeks ago when I had discovered he'd worked the system to free a suspected killer. A killer who had killed again...the father of my client.

I had serious issues with that. I knew that Kingsley was doing his job. I get it. But it didn't mean I had to respect it or like it.

To Kingsley's credit he hadn't pushed the issue with me. Mostly, he had sat back and waited for me to work through my issues. And to my own credit, I knew enough not to make a rash decision. Too many people act too quickly, end relationships too quickly. Better to be clear about what you want.

I wasn't clear yet; I was still conflicted.

But now wasn't the time for that. I had had a long day and an even longer night, and now all I wanted was a warm hug, a warm smile, and a warm body.

It was no surprise that Kingsley came immediately to mind, although I had flirted with the idea of contacting Fang. The idea didn't stick. Fang was a whole new jigsaw puzzle of confusion that I still needed to piece together, and I just wasn't up to it, not now. Not with everything else going on.

Kingsley, although a bastard, was familiar and loveable and warm as hell.

The banging in the kitchen stopped, and a few moments later Franklin appeared in the living room with a tray of drinks. He set a goblet in front of each of us and stood back. Franklin wasn't happy. He was also a piece of work. Literally. The man, I was certain, had been pieced together from many different men. Where Kingsley met him, I didn't know. Why such a creature served as a werewolf's butler, I couldn't imagine. But there was a hell of a story here, somewhere. Kingsley had promised he would tell me the butler's tale. Someday. And if and when I was done being pissed at Kingsley, maybe I would finally hear it.

"Is that all?" asked the butler. His slightly melodic accent was nearly impossible to place. It could have been British, but it wasn't any British accent I had ever heard. The words *Old English* came to mind, too. As in old, *old* English. This, I'm certain, was a psychic hit, but I could have been wrong. Just how old Franklin was remained to be seen.

"Thank you, Franklin. That will be all," said Kingsley, waving him off.

The butler nodded. "If you and the lady need anything else, please do not hesitate to rouse me from a deep and satisfying sleep."

"We won't, Franklin. Now, off you go!"

Franklin bowed and turned and loped off, his legs seemingly not quite working together. Almost as if they had been two different legs from two different bodies. A theory that I was beginning to accept.

Kingsley reached for his wine. "Drink up, dear."

I reached for my own drink, but it wasn't wine. It was chilled hemoglobin, and if I didn't hurry and drink, the surface layer would coagulate.

I picked the cold glass up with both hands and brought it to my nose, inhaling deeply the strong coppery scent. Metallic, rich, alive. I brought the goblet to my lips and that first dribble of blood sent a shiver through me that was akin to a smoker's high.

It had taken me a long, long time to actually acquire a taste for blood. To actually enjoy it. But it depended on the blood. The finer the plasma, the more I enjoyed it. The purer the hemoglobin, the better the experience. The more pleasurable the experience. The more beneficial, too. Fine blood gave me extra energy, added strength, and a better life experience.

But my blood of choice—or of necessity—comes from a butchery in nearby Norco, where I had a running account with them. Once a week they delivered the stuff to my door, no questions asked, although they believed it was for scientific purposes. The blood was often filled with fur and skin and other floaties that I couldn't quite place. Didn't *want* to place. It was utterly disgusting, but it nourished me and no doubt kept me alive.

This blood was different. This blood was heavenly. This blood, I was certain, was from a human. There were no impurities in it. It was silky smooth and fresh and filled with a life force that absolutely electrified me.

"Thirsty?" asked Kingsley.

I opened my eyes. I found myself staring into the empty goblet, whose interior was coated now with a thin film of blood.

"Very," I said. "Would you think less of me if I licked the inside?"

"Waste not, want not, I say."

I ran my tongue inside, licking hungrily, and only then did I realize how ghoulish I looked. "Did that look as ghoulish as I think it did?" I asked.

He grinned. "Worse."

"Great." But that didn't stop me from using my index finger to swipe at the last few drops of blood.

Kingsley watched me with a bemused expression. He was wearing a robe and not much else. His legs were hairy as hell, but also roped with muscle. His toes, I saw, were extraordinarily long. And hairy, too. He wiggled them at me when he saw me looking at them. They looked like ten frightened mice.

"I'm getting more and more used to drinking blood," I said.

"It was bound to happen."

"I mean, I'll always hate the animal blood, but this human blood was nearly orgasmic."

"Do you feel stronger?"

"In every way, but it's late, or early, and I feel myself getting tired."

"No worries. The blood will more than sustain you for a few days. Much more so than that polluted pig and cow crap you drink."

I had experienced this before. Human blood revitalized me unlike anything else. So much so that I realized that I was *meant* to drink human blood. I was meant—designed—to kill humans.

"So whose blood is this?" I asked.

"Do you really want to know?"

"No. Yes. Shit."

Kingsley got up, and as he did so, he flashed me the goods. Whether he meant to or not, I don't know...but holy sweet Jesus. Did I really just see that? My God, how did he walk around with that thing?

Kingsley, defense attorney, werewolf—and now, apparently, *pervert*—sat next to me and gave no indication that he had just given me the mother of all peep shows.

"I'm going to let you in on a little secret," he said, and knocked back the rest of his wine like it was booze-flavored Kool-Aide.

"It's not a secret," I said. "And it ain't little."

"Excuse me?"

"Never mind."

But I caught the smallest of shit-eating grins on his face.

"Go on," I said, shaking my head. "And this time try to keep the robe closed."

"I do my best to keep it closed."

I patted his meaty knee. "Well, do better, big boy. Now, what is it that's such a big secret?"

He sat back, but this time he kept the robe closed well enough. "The blood is from a donor, Sam."

"A donor?"

He nodded.

"A willing donor?" I prodded.

"Willing enough," he said.

"I don't like the sound of that."

"It's not as bad as it seems."

"But it's still bad?"

"Gruesome, perhaps. Macabre."

"Perhaps you should just tell me what you know."

"There's a world of vampires out there, Sam, that you haven't been introduced to yet. At least, I don't think you have."

I thought back to Detective Hanner. Whether or not she was a vampire, I didn't know, and I most certainly hadn't been officially introduced to other vampires.

The defense attorney went on. "You're not the only one of your kind, Sam, and the vampire who attacked you wasn't the last."

Knowing this set off alarm bells within me. I didn't like knowing there were others like me, truth be known. I knew *me*. And I trusted me. I didn't trust others. "How many more are there?" I asked.

"Not many; in fact, very few."

"Are we talking thousands?"

"Hundreds, perhaps. Scattered around the world."

And yet there were two in Fullerton, I mused, but didn't say anything. The one who had attacked me (and was subsequently killed by a vampire hunter a few months back...the same hunter who later came looking for me), and now perhaps Detective Hanner. If you add me into the mix, that's three in Orange County alone. Hell, three in Fullerton alone.

Kingsley went on: "There's a larger than normal grouping of vamps here in Southern California; particularly Los Angeles."

"I might have met one."

"Who?"

I hesitated, wondering if I might be giving away Detective Hanner's secret. After all, I wasn't sure if there couldn't be some weird, age-old vampire/werewolf feud going on. (And if there was, why hadn't I gotten the memo?)

Kingsley reached over and laid his warm hand on my knee. I inwardly sighed. I craved warmth. And other than the snuggling hugs of my kids, the warmth from a man was the next best.

He said, "Don't worry, Sam. Many of the local vampires are friends of mine."

"Friends?"

"Close acquaintances. We sort of naturally gravitate to each other."

"And there's no, like, war or something going

on?"

He chuckled. "War?"

"You know, like on *Twilight* or *Underworld*."

He squeezed my knee a little. "And what would we be fighting over?"

"Dominion over the earth? The blood of humanity?"

"There are others who control the earth, Sam, and they are very human. And, hell, even I'm afraid of them."

I told him about the Fullerton detective. As I did, Kingsley nodded and smiled. "An old friend."

"How old?"

"Older than you and I combined. Anyway, Hanner, like other immortals, has taken precautions to discreetly blend in with society."

"So they don't run around killing people."

"Not as often as you would think."

I said, "And that's where the donors come in."

"Right."

"And who are these donors?" I asked.

"Selected humans."

"And how are they selected?"

"Most are lovers. Some are enemies. And a few are simply unfortunate enough to have crossed paths with a hungry vampire."

"Do these donors know they are donating to real vampires?"

"My guess would be yes and no. Perhaps a few of the more trusted ones do."

"And the others?"

"The others are, I imagine, giving their blood most unwillingly."

"Then why call them 'donors'?"

"It sounds better, don't you think?"

I turned the empty goblet in my hand. What little of the red stuff remained had long since dried. I suddenly felt sick to my stomach. So whose blood had this belonged to? I may never know.

A sudden wave of weakness hit me. The sun was coming. "I need a place to crash," I said.

"Mi bed es su bed."

"That's some of the worst Spanish I've ever heard."

He squeezed my knee harder. "I'm getting up now anyway. You can have the bed to yourself."

My heart sank a little.

"Is something wrong, Sam?"

I still hadn't forgiven Kingsley, but I did miss his touch. "Would you..." I paused, then tried again. "Would you lay with me until I fall asleep?"

He smiled brightly. "Would be my pleasure. And I'll wake Franklin up and have him vampire-treat the windows with some blankets or something."

"Oh, great," I said, as the first wave of exhaustion hit me. "Give him even more reason to hate me."

Chapter Thirty-six

Although I generally need to crank my alarm clock as loud as it gets to rouse me from my sleep, I found myself emerging from the blackest of depths at the sound of my cell phone ringing.

By the fourth ring, I was almost alive again.

By the fifth, I had fumbled for it on Kingsley's nightstand. I had a brief glimpse of the time: 10:18 a.m. I also had a brief glimpse of the caller: Aaron King, the old L.A. detective with the killer smile.

I answered the phone. At least, I think I answered the phone. I touched a button on the cell and hoped for the best.

"Hello?"

"Did you just say 'hello'?" said Aaron King.

"I think so, yes."

"You sound like a dying frog."

"You're closer than you think."

"I've got news," he said.

"Don't tell me you've been working all night."

"There's no rest for the wicked. Besides, I don't sleep well these days."

I sat up a little straighter. Kingsley, I saw, was long gone. The shades in the room had been drawn tight. A blanket, a bed comforter perhaps, had also been hung over a small window above the bed. And it had been hung neatly, too. Franklin might not like me very much, but he did good work.

I said, "What's your news?"

"I just got a call from a kid in Buena Park. He recognized our guy on the flyer. Apparently, Lauren and Maddie's friend is a big-time drug runner and all-around scary man."

"You should see me trembling. What else does our contact know?"

"The guy's name is Carl Luck. Known drug dealer and pornographer."

"Mommy would be proud."

"Last our contact heard, Mr. Luck lives in Simi Valley."

"The porn capital of the world."

"You say that like it's a bad thing."

"Eww," I said. "Is that all?"

"Nope. It gets better."

"I love better."

"Apparently Carl Luck drinks and gambles at an Indian casino near Simi, called Moon Feathers."

"A fitting name."

"I thought so," he said. "Anyway, I did a background check on Carl Luck."

"And?"

"And nothing."

I thought about that. "Maybe that's not his real name."

"Maybe it's his gambling *nom de plume*."

"Better than calling yourself Carl Loser."

I could almost see King grin on his end of the line.

"Anyway, his name doesn't matter," I said. "He could call himself Pepé Le Pew for all I care. Just as long as he shows up at Moon Feathers."

"Don't forget the part about him being a bad man. Remember, there's a very good chance that he killed Maddie's mother. And don't give me that shit about you being a highly trained federal agent."

"I'm a highly trained federal agent, I'll be fine."

"Shit." He paused, then added. "I want to come with you. Maybe bring the boys as back ups."

I shook my head even though Aaron couldn't see me shaking my head. "No. I want to go alone. I'll be fine. Promise."

He didn't like it, and I didn't blame him. I wouldn't have liked it either. The truth was, the boys just might get in the way. He said, "I'll keep my phone handy. Call me if you need anything."

"I will."

"Promise me."

"Scout's honor."

He laughed harder. "Okay, a federal agent I believe, but I *know* you weren't a Boy Scout."

We fell into silence and I felt that there was something heavy on Aaron's heart. I waited for him. Twenty seconds later he spoke, and I sensed it was after much deliberation. "I saw you looking at me last night."

I waited, sensing where this would go.

"I know that look," he said.

"And what look is that?"

"Recognition," he said simply.

Just outside the bedroom, I heard the sounds of someone cleaning: items on a table being moved and then being replaced again. I knew Kingsley didn't use a house cleaner. It was just Franklin. The idea of catching the gangly, patchwork man using a feather duster almost made me laugh.

"What do you mean?" I asked, although I was certain I knew perfectly well what he meant.

"You know who I am."

"Oh?"

"Don't play coy with me, kiddo. I saw the look in your eyes last night. How did you know?"

Now I heard Franklin humming to himself. Humming and dusting. A man composed of perhaps a dozen different men. I had Frankenstein outside my door, and Elvis on the phone.

My life is weird.

"I know things," I said.

"How?"

"Some call it a gift. I don't know what to call it."

"Are we talking ESP or something?"

"Yeah, something like that."

"So then there's no secrets from you."

"Often, no, although I can't always control the psychic hits I get," I said.

I could almost see him nodding to himself at the other end of the line. He said, "I know a thing or two about secrets, lil' lady, especially after keeping such a big one for so long."

"I bet," I said, although I didn't like where this was going.

He paused, then said, "And you have a big one yourself."

"No comment," I said.

He chuckled lightly into the mouthpiece. "Call me if you need any help. Psychic or not, I don't like the idea of you heading out to that casino alone."

"I can take care of myself."

"Maybe," he said, and now he didn't bother to disguise his voice. A harmonious and deep southern twang came through, edged with age, but as familiar as apple pie. He said, "Either way, lil' mama, let's get a coffee some time and talk about secrets."

"Sounds like a plan," I said, and shivered. I felt like a teenager at her first concert. An Elvis concert, no less.

He chuckled lightly and hung up.

Chapter Thirty-seven

It was early afternoon, and I was sitting next to my son's bed. The blinds were drawn tight, but I was still feeling weak and miserable and utterly exhausted.

I shouldn't be awake. I should be asleep in the dark.

Of course, whether or not I actually sleep is still an unanswered question. A few years ago, just after my attack and back when Danny was still making an effort to be a supportive husband, we had done an experiment. He had watched me closely while I slept. His conclusion (and he had looked seriously rattled when he had reported this), was that I didn't appear to be moving or breathing or even alive. That I had looked like a corpse in a morgue.

Hell, that might have been when I started losing him.

Speaking of Danny, he had waited here until my arrival, and had then given me a long and creepy hug that had included a little pelvic thrust that made me want to vomit.

I mean, what the hell was that? Our son is lying in a hospital bed and he's coming on to me?

It had taken all my willpower not to drive my knee up into said groin. He then patted my shoulder, gave me a pathetic puppy dog look with a crooked grin, and then quickly departed. After all, he had ambulances to chase.

I shuddered again.

Some errant sunlight from an opening in the window splashed across the far wall, and just looking at it seemed to have an ill effect on me. Sunlight, quite simply, drained me. It also physically hurt like hell, which led me to believe that if I were exposed to it long enough, without protection, I had every reason to believe I would die a very painful and miserable death.

So much for being immortal.

My son had yet to stir. Nurses had come and gone. All of whom smiled sadly at me, although most tried to lift my spirits. For a boy to lie unconscious this long, for a boy to be this sick, for a boy to have doctors this concerned, well, things did not look good for a loving mama, and they knew it.

Still, they smiled and said kind things, and I nodded and accepted their words, and when they were gone, I wept.

I was not weeping when Detective Sherbet

stepped into the room. The big guy came bearing gifts, and the sight of him daintily holding the string of a helium-filled balloon in one hand and clutching a fistful of flowers in the other was enough to make my heart smile. He stood there blinking, eyes adjusting to the gloom.

And while he blinked and adjusted, I eased off the bed and crossed the room and threw my arms around the detective in a move that I think surprised him.

"Excuse me, ma'am, but am I in the right place?" he asked.

"Most definitely," I said. I was still hugging him. God, he was so warm...and thick around the middle. Just the way I liked it.

"You do realize that you are still hugging me," he said, but I felt him switch the balloon over and then use his free hand to pat me gently on the head.

I couldn't speak. Instead, a big choking sob burst out of me and I hugged him harder than I had hugged anyone before, and my tears quickly stained his shirt.

Chapter Thirty-eight

Hidden in the crook of his arm, previously unnoticed, had been a big, greasy bag of donuts.

We were now sitting across from each other at the foot of my son's bed. The smell of the greasy donut was both delicious and nauseating. Sherbet was currently working on a maple old fashioned. Some of the frosting broke off and had sprinkled down his shirt and over his thick thigh. He ignored the frosting crumbs. I thought they looked delicious.

"I'd offer you one," he said. "Except I know you'll say no."

"Thanks anyway, but I'm not hungry."

"Gee, how did I know you were going to say that?" he asked between bites.

"Because anyone who cared an ounce about their bodies wouldn't put that crap in it." Which was a lie. I loved donuts. I just couldn't eat them...or anything, for that matter.

"Except for those whose bodies are indestructible," said Sherbet off-handedly.

My heart slammed hard against my ribs. *Sweet, Jesus, what did Sherbet know?*

He stopped chewing and looked at me curiously. "You look like you just saw a ghost. Relax, my doctor tells me my heart has no business being as strong as it is."

I breathed again. *Good lord.*

I said, "And so you figure you might as well push your heart to the limit?"

"Not really," he said, sucking on his fingers. "I just like donuts."

I shook my head while he dug into the bag, coming up with something pink and sprinkled. He said, "I've grown rather fond of these donuts."

"And how's your son, by the way?" I asked.

Sherbet looked at me from over the donut. "I bring out a pink donut and it immediately reminds you of my son?"

"Yes and no."

He chomped into it. Pink frosting coated his thick, cop mustache. "He's fine, of course. I love him terribly, but there's something definitely wrong."

"Wrong how?"

"I keep catching him in his mother's clothing, especially her shoes."

"Is it that you catch him, or he likes to wear them?"

"Both, I think. Makes me want to cry."

We were silent, and as the wall clock behind me ticked so loudly that I could practically hear the inner gears grinding together, Sherbet figured out what an ass he was being.

"Look, I'm sorry," he said. "You've got your little one here fighting for his life and I'm bitching because mine likes to dress up like Nanny McPhee."

I nodded, said nothing.

Sherbet reached out and placed his warm hand over my own. He took mine tightly and didn't flinch from the cold. I think he was getting used to my icy hands.

"Let's change the subject, okay?" he suggested.

I nodded again and looked away. I wasn't going to cry. I was tired of crying.

He said, "The guy you found dead in the meth house was murdered."

"I'm shocked and outraged," I said. I was neither, of course. Drug hits were common and quickly forgotten by the police.

"Execution style, too."

"Do we care enough about him to know his name?" I asked.

"No," said Sherbet. "We don't. He was a known user and dealer. Too many suspects, too little time. The place was grand central station for meth and blow...and other things as well."

"Prostitutes," I said.

"And various child abuses that we need not get into here."

"Let's call it for what it is, detective. Child slavery and prostitution."

The detective looked sick. I felt sick, too. He nodded gravely and dropped the unfinished donut in his bag. It's hard to have an appetite for pink donuts when the talk turns to child abuse.

He said, "From what we understand, the children are used as...payments, of one sort or another."

I nodded, and felt bile rise in the back of my throat.

Sherbet continued, "Maddie's mother was no doubt caught up in it. And now she's dead, apparently."

"And little Maddie is alone," I said.

Sherbet nodded and we were silent. He turned to me. "You making any headway on the case?"

"Some," I said. I decided not to mention Aaron's hot lead in Simi Valley. Mostly because I didn't trust the police enough at this point to get Maddie out alive, wherever she was. I trusted Sherbet, certainly, but he was only one man, and Simi Valley was not his beat, not by a long shot.

"Let me know if you need some help," he said.

"You bet."

Sherbet was openly staring at me.

"What?" I said.

"I was just thinking."

"Don't hurt yourself, Detective."

He ignored me. "It's funny how suspects keep ending up dead on cases you investigate."

"Whatever do you mean, Detective?"

"You were working an angle on the Jerry Blum case last month."

"You know this how?"

"I have friends in the FBI, too, Sam."

"Good for you."

"You were making inquiries for your client. A Stuart something-or-other."

"Stuart Young."

"Whatever. Anyway, Jerry Blum has been missing for a month."

"Maybe he's on the lam."

"Or maybe he's dead," said Sherbet.

I shrugged.

"Well, let's try to keep the body count down this time, Sam."

"People die," I said. "Especially bad people."

"I'll pretend I didn't hear that."

My son made a small sound and turned over in his sleep. As he turned, the black shadow that surrounded him turned with him. My heart sank further.

Sherbet patted me on the shoulder and stood. He looked down at me long and hard, and then left.

Chapter Thirty-nine

You there, Moon Dance?

It was Fang via a text message. With our super-secret identities now revealed, we had graduated from anonymous IM messages to exchanging our cell numbers and texting like real people. Or, at least, like teenagers.

I was still sitting next to my son. It was coming on noon and I was weak and sad and tired.

Hi, Fang. :(

There was a slight delay, perhaps a minute. Texting wasn't as fast as IMing.

Why are you sad, Moon Dance?

It's my son.

You mentioned he was sick. Is he not better?

Worse, I wrote, paused, and then added: *He's dying.*

That was all I could write. And even writing those two words was nearly impossible. The words seemed so unlikely, implausible, unreal. More so than my own vampirism. How could my healthy, happy, quirky little boy be dying?

Outside the room, a doctor rushed quickly by. I heard shouting from somewhere. Two orderlies quickly followed behind. Doctors risked their lives more than people realized.

You would never say that lightly, wrote Fang. *So it must be true.*

I spent the next few minutes catching him up to date on my son's health and the black halo surrounding his body.

There was a long period of silence from my phone, which I had set to vibrate. I adjusted my weight on my hip and reached out and stroked my son's face. He was burning up.

The phone vibrated. *Do the doctors know what's wrong with him?*

They're saying it could be Kawasaki's Disease. Hold on.

And I knew Fang was looking up the disease. I ran my fingers through my son's hair for the next five minutes. My phone buzzed again.

There's only a 2% mortality rate, Fang wrote.

2% is enough, I wrote.

I'm sorry, Moon Dance. I wish there was something I could do.

I was about to write to him, when another message appeared from Fang. It was simple and to the point:

Actually, Moon Dance, I think I know of a way

to save your son.
    Don't go anywhere! I'm calling you.

Chapter Forty

I was outside of St. Jude's, huddled under the eve of the main entrance, as deep in the shadows as I could be. Still, I could literally feel my skin burning.

I could give a damn about my skin.

Fang answered my call immediately. "Hello, Moon Dance."

I found myself pacing, turning small circles in front of the hospital entrance. The automatic door kept sliding open. The information nurse working the front desk gave me a nasty look. I ignored her.

"Talk to me, Fang."

"I'm talking," he said, and I could hear the excitement in his voice. "There is a way to save your son."

"What way?"

And the moment I asked the question, I knew the answer. Fang and I were deeply connected and I either picked up on his thoughts or intuited his meaning. I think I gasped and nearly choked.

"No," I said. "No fucking way. I'm not doing it."

"You read my mind, Moon Dance."

"Of course I read your fucking mind. I have to sit."

There was an alabaster bench just inside the shade that I would risk, and as I sat, I regretted doing so almost immediately. I could practically smell my burning skin, despite my long sleeves and heavy sunscreen.

I ignored the pain and buried my face in my hands. People were looking at me, sure, but a grieving mother outside of a children's hospital wasn't anything new.

But a grieving mother contemplating giving her son eternal life was another matter altogether.

I said, "I can't do it, Fang. I could never do that to him. How could you even suggest that?"

"You didn't let me finish. Or, for that matter, speak, since you read my thoughts."

Yes, I knew there was more. I knew he was eager to continue with this, but my own wildly spinning emotions prevented me from picking up on his additional thoughts. In fact, they still did.

"Go ahead," I said.

"The medallion, Moon Dance."

And that's all he needed to say; in an instant I knew what he meant and what he was getting at.

The medallion, or amulet. Or whatever it was.

Worn by my attacker six years ago, and hand-delivered to me by the vampire hunter who killed him.

The medallion, that, according to Kingsley, could *reverse* vampirism.

Fang was speaking, but I was having a hell of a time focusing. He said, "Heal him with vampirism, Moon Dance, and then return him to mortality with the medallion."

"But how?" I said. "How does it work?"

"I don't know...but someone out there does."

"I gotta go," I said suddenly, and clicked off.

Chapter Forty-one

Kingsley Fulcrum had a new secretary. No surprise there since I watched the last one die a few months ago, shot to death by none other than Detective Sherbet. And, since killing together has a way of bonding people, perhaps that's why the good detective and I got along so swimmingly.

It was a working theory.

This new secretary wasn't as sexy as the last. Which was probably a good thing. Maybe after a century or more, the big bad wolf was finally learning to keep it in his pants, or tucked away in his fur.

Anyway, this slightly older and plainer secretary (although still cute in her ruffled cardigan sweater) told me that Kingsley was with a client. Kingsley's clients were often murderers with a lot of money.

I could give a fuck about his clients.

As I marched past her and down a hallway, I heard her rapidly punching buttons on the intercom. She must have successfully buzzed Kingsley, because as I threw open his door he was just reaching for the phone with what appeared to be a look of irritation. The mighty attorney didn't like to be disturbed, apparently. The look of irritation quickly turned to one of dumbfounded shock when he saw me.

The big guy cleaned up well. He was looking absolutely debonair in a black Armani suit, a pair of over-the-top and beyond stylish Berluti shoes, and hair so slicked back that a girl might break a nail scratching behind his ears.

Unless that girl, of course, was a vampire.

"Sam," he said, standing slowly from behind his desk. "This isn't a good time."

His client turned to me. Another man dressed in a nice suit. A man who looked bored and rich and entitled. Okay, it's hard to look entitled, but that was the feeling I was getting from him. I also got a very strong hit that he was a murderer. A cold-blooded murderer. I got another hit...he had strangled his own wife in her sleep. I heard her last strangled gasps as I stood there in the doorway and he sat there looking bored.

Sweet Jesus my hits were getting stronger and stronger.

I walked over to the guy and pulled him out of his chair. He didn't go willingly. He tried to push my hands away but couldn't. As I pulled him out of his chair, Kingsley ran from around his desk, his Armani suit *swooshing*.

"Hey!" shouted the guy as I held him in front of me.

Kingsley shouted something similar.

The guy tried again to shove me away, but I wasn't going anywhere. I had him by the collar of his nice suit. And now that he was on his feet, I slammed his face hard onto the table.

"You killed her, you worthless piece of shit. You strangled her in her sleep, you fucking coward, and then you lit a Cuban cigar after a job well done. An *illegal* Cuban cigar."

He struggled to get up, but I held him down on the table and all the anger and frustration and pain and confusion and despair I had felt over the past few days came flooding out of me. I lifted his face and slammed it again into the table. Blood immediately pooled around his eye socket. I had split the skin along his upper orbital ridge. Poor baby.

"I will personally see to it that you rot in hell, you fucking—"

And that's when Kingsley pulled me off the man. Kicking and screaming, I didn't go willingly. But Kingsley happened to be one hell of a strong guy.

Chapter Forty-two

"What the hell was that, Sam?"

I was sitting in an empty side office. Apparently, Kingsley Fulcrum made so much blood money representing rich, murderous scumbags that he could afford to have empty offices.

"What was what?" I asked. I was still fuming, and I was having a hard time looking Kingsley in the eye. The big son-of-a-bitch was really bothering me these days. I had come here for a completely different reason, but I had let my emotions get the better of me.

Hey, I'm only human.

Or something.

"Playing Whack-A-Mole with my client's head, Sam. That's what."

"Whack-A-Mole?" I asked, and I started laughing, nearly hysterically, and then I was crying, definitely hysterically, harder than I had in quite a long time. Kingsley stood apart from me, watching me, and then he came over and gave me a big hug, wrapping those huge arms around me, patting my back and rubbing my shoulders, and telling me everything would be okay.

***

I was calmer. We were back in Kingsley's office, minus the murderous scumbag, who had apparently left holding a bag of ice to his face. Someone had cleaned the blood off the table, although I could still smell the sharp hemoglobin radiating off the freshly polished wood surface. Must be the vampire in me.

My stomach growled, and I hated myself for that.

"You can't keep killing my clients, Sam," said Kingsley. His right butt cheek was sitting on the corner of his desk. I was sitting in one of his client chairs. Everywhere around me were depictions of moons: moon photographs, paperweights, lamps. Even a moon screen saver. The moon bookends, each by itself a half moon, seemed to be the newest additions to his office.

Yeah, the man had a moon obsession, which stands to reason. His obsession was also how he had found me in the phone book so many months ago. Under "Moon", of course.

"Well, your clients are scumbags," I said.

"Be that as it may, they deserve a fair trial."

"Whatever helps you sleep at night, big guy."

"Why are you here, Sam?"

I stared at him...no doubt icily. He calmly returned my gaze. We did this for about ten seconds before I finally lowered my eyes and looked away. "I'm sorry," I said. "That wasn't cool. I guess I'm desperate."

"A desperate vampire is a sight to see."

"A desperate mother is worse."

He nodded and eased off the corner of his desk. He sat next to me and adjusted the drape of his pants. Kingsley, as always, smelled of fine cologne and that special something else. Something wild. He waited. As he waited, I gathered my thoughts.

Finally, I said, "The medallion that's in my possession..."

He looked at me sideways, turning his head just a fraction of an inch. "What about it?"

"Is it really true that it can reverse vampirism?"

Although I wasn't looking at him, I knew he had narrowed his eyes. Kingsley was nearly impossible for me to read psychically. I wondered if it was like that for all other immortals, too.

He said, "That's the legend about it."

"What else do you know about it?"

"I know that a lot of people are looking for it."

"People? Or vampires?"

"Vampires are people, too," he said, grinning easily. And then he grew serious. "Why, Sam?"

The smell of blood wafting up from the desk was diminishing. The growling in my stomach subsided accordingly. I told Kingsley about my plan, minus any references to Fang. There was no need to make the big werewolf jealous. Fang might be a freaky dude, but he was no physical match for Kingsley. At least, not presently.

Make me into a vampire, Moon Dance.

Yeah, I still haven't forgotten those words.

Anyway, I laid the plan out to Kingsley, and as I did so, he leaned a meaty elbow against the chair's arm and took me in, watching me closely as I spoke. And as I spoke, I couldn't help but notice that the slight amber in his eyes caught some of the office lighting and reflected it back to me twofold. Tenfold. He can look so wild sometimes.

When I was done talking, Kingsley's reply was instant and heart breaking: "I don't like it, Sam."

"What's not to like?" I said, jumping up. I paced behind him. "I save my son and later, I return him to being human. It's perfect."

He was shaking his head, and the amber glow was gone from his eyes, replaced with something close to alarm. And also something else. Concern. "Unless it doesn't work, Sam."

"But why wouldn't it work?" I heard the desperation in my voice, which had risen an octave or two. I spun on Kingsley, standing before him.

"Because it's just a story, Sam. A legend."

"All legends have some basis of truth. Look at us. And quit looking at me that way."

"What way?"

"Like I've lost my mind."

He stood suddenly and towered over me. "I don't think you've lost your mind, but I think you're desperate, and dangerous, and if you would for one second listen to yourself you would see how scary you sound."

I looked up at him as he looked down at me. He was breathing hard, and I could hear his heart thumping through his wide chest. "Who do I need to talk to?" I asked. "Who would know more about the medallion?"

He looked at me long and hard. "Sam, please."

"I'm going to do whatever it takes to save my son, goddammit."

"Even if it means turning him into a monster, Sam? Even if it means draining the blood from his body? And what if you can't turn him back? What then, Sam?"

I heard footsteps just outside Kingsley's office door. His new secretary was there. How much she'd heard, I didn't know, but I suspected his doors were quite thick. If anything, she was concerned for her boss's welfare.

I said nothing. How could anyone answer that question? Hell, has that question ever been posed before? Ever? In the history of mankind?

Kingsley continued, "I'll tell you what would happen if you *can't* change him back, Sam. Your son will be undead, like you. He will feed on blood, like you. He will be a monster."

"Like me?"

"For all eternity, Sam. Your boy. Your little

boy. Don't do this to him, Sam. You can't take this chance."

I held his gaze long and hard. "Who do I talk to, Kingsley?"

He took in a lot of air, crossed his arms, and looked away. "Let me ask around, Sam."

I nodded and felt a combination of joy and dread, fear and hope. "Thank you," I said.

But he didn't answer me or look at me, and shortly after that I left his office.

Chapter Forty-three

I had just slipped into my car after practically sprinting across the baking asphalt when my phone rang. Gasping and in real pain, I looked at the faceplate:

Caller Unknown.

Heart thumping and still reeling from my singed skin, I clicked on the phone.

"Hello," I said. My face and hands were on fire, despite the copious amounts of sunscreen—and a sunhat that was wide enough to shade a small Balkan country.

"Hi," said the tiny voice, a voice that was somehow even tinier than I remembered.

"Maddie!"

"You know my name."

"Of course I know your name, honey." But as much as I wanted to comfort her and reassure her, I needed information. "Maddie, honey, how many people live with you?"

"Two grownup men now."

"Are they black or white?"

"Both. The white man is new. He's really mean."

Maddie had a slight lisp and it was the most precious sound I had ever heard. I absently started my car and turned my air conditioner full blast on me, while huddling as far away from any sunlight as I could. My van's side windows were equipped with pull-down shades, which I rarely, if ever, pulled up. The windshield sunshade was still in place, blocking most of the sun, although laser-like beams still found their way through here and there.

So there was a black guy and a white guy. The white guy, I knew, could have been Hispanic or even Asian. Maddie was only five. I doubted she saw race and color like an older child would. Or as an adult would.

Sherbet had confirmed the worst, that some kind of child swapping was going on. Children for drugs. Children for money. Children for sex. A slave trade where lives meant little, and no doubt most kids disappeared or ended up dead. Along with the mothers.

"Maddie, honey, are you in a house?"

"A house?"

"Or is it an apartment?"

"Peoples live here. We take the vader."

The vader? My head was swimming. Jesus, I had had my questions rehearsed for when and if I heard from Maddie again, but now all my questions had gone out the window.

Think. Focus.

"Honey, what can you see from the window? Can you see anything?"

There was a slight pause. I heard her pushing aside what sounded like blinds. "I see a big house."

"Where?"

"It's high on top of the biggest mountain I've ever seen!"

My heart started hammering. I knew Simi Valley. The federal agency I had worked for, HUD, used a facility outside of the city to hold seminars and training. The facility was away from prying eyes, up against the base of a majestic, sweeping mountain range. Or, perhaps, a very big hill. Certainly big enough to call a mountain if you were a small girl from the streets of Buena Park.

And at the top of the hill, majestically overlooking the city was a museum. Not quite a mansion, but it looks like one from a distance.

The Ronald Reagan Museum.

The Moon Feather Indian casino, if I recalled correctly, wasn't too far away from our training facility, either.

She's in Simi Valley. I knew it. I felt it in every fiber of my being.

I also sensed something else. Or, rather *someone* else. And from somewhere over the phone line, I heard what sounded like a door slam followed by a man's yell. The yell sounded drunken and angry.

"I have to go," said Maddie, whispering into the mouthpiece. Her whisper sounded nearly as loud as her little voice.

The line dropped before I could say goodbye.

Chapter Forty-four

I was back at the hospital, sitting in a chair at the foot of my son's bed. He was sleeping quietly. Too quietly. I would have thought he was dead if not for the hospital equipment that chirped out a heart beat.

The dark halo around him was bigger than ever. My son, to my eyes, seemed lost in a cloud of black smoke.

Sitting on my lap was a clipboard with a mostly blank sheet of paper I had found in the backseat of my car. The paper had my daughter's name on it and the beginning of an assignment. I wondered idly if she ever finished the assignment.

I held in my hand a Pilot Gel Ink Rolling Ball pen, which I preferred to use when I did my automatic writing sessions.

Automatic writing is still new to me. In fact, I'd only done it a couple of times, and both times I was certain I was going crazy.

In essence, as it was initially explained to me by Fang (and verified by a little online research) the process of automatic writing is a way to communicate with the spirit world. In particular, with highly evolved enlightened beings who know what the hell they're talking about.

At least, that was the idea.

Who or what came through in these sessions was certainly open to debate. And, yes, there was a part of me that seriously suspected I was moving my own hand, and giving myself the answers I wanted to hear.

Just a part of me.

The other part of me, perhaps the part that was still human, believed that I was getting messages from beyond. By spirit guides, or spiritual beings.

Or, for all I knew, Jim Morrison, unless he was alive, too, and working as a bounty hunter in Hawaii.

I went through the various steps of centering myself, imagining silver cords attaching themselves to my ankles and lower spine and reaching down through the many hospital floors, the building's foundation, through the very ground itself, down through Hell and a lost world of dinosaurs, and all the way to the center of the earth, where I mentally tied them tightly around three massive boulders.

Now firmly anchored, I closed my eyes and attempted to empty my mind by focusing on the physical act of breathing, drawing air in through my nose and out my mouth, even if it was air I didn't need. Except I kept thinking about my son, lying there just a few feet away, fighting for his life.

Focus, Sam.

I closed my eyes and, as I breathed, I pictured the stale, medicinal hospital air flowing over my lips and down deep into my lungs. I breathed in, holding the air, and then exhaled it.

I did this over and over, breathing and picturing, and any time I thought of my son, I gently released the thought.

In and out, in and out.

Breathe, breathe.

My hand twitched.

I kept reminding myself to breathe, and as I breathed I imagined the air currents tinged with gold, and the golden air flowing into my mouth and filling me with golden light.

My hand twitched again, followed by a full-blown spasm.

The pen gripped in my fingers moved back and forth.

It's coming, I thought. Whatever it is.

Keep breathing. Breathing. In and out. Golden light.

Jesus, my hand is moving.

Don't think about it. Good, good.

But now I couldn't deny that something seemed to have settled in me. I actually felt another presence. A warm and loving presence.

And then my hand moved again, and again, and

I realized it was writing. I looked down at my clipboard as two words appeared:

Hello, Samantha.

Chapter Forty-five

"Hello," I said quietly, feeling slightly silly, but also feeling like something very important, and very exciting, was happening. "Um, how are you?" I added lamely.

My hand twitched again and again, and it kept on twitching until it wrote out a reply. I could only watch in stunned silence. My hand, in these moments, did not feel like my own.

I'm doing very well, it wrote. *It's a great day to be alive, is it not?*

I thought of my son, and a great pain filled my heart. I had come here now to ask about Anthony, but suddenly I wasn't sure I really wanted to hear the answers.

My son was showing signs of stabilizing. This should be good news, but it wasn't. Not to me. I knew better. His black halo was growing. How do you convince a doctor that you need a second or third opinion when the patient seems to be responding to treatments?

Responding for now. I knew that would all change.

I had called children's hospital after children's hospital, burning up my phone, demanding to speak to other infectious disease specialists. Few would speak to me, and those who did were generally guarded. I begged them to come see my boy, that I felt something was very, very wrong, and they reassured me that my son's doctor was one of the best in the business.

One specialist in Chicago told me he would look into it, and later called to tell me that he was flying in to see my son. I thanked him profusely, crying nearly hysterically, but in my heart of hearts, I knew he would fail.

Modern medicine would fail. I needed a miracle. And thanks to Fang, I had an idea what that miracle might entail.

For now, though, I simply said, "Am I really alive?" My voice was barely above a whisper. "There are some who believe that beings such as myself are dead."

More twitching and tingling. More writing. *Do you feel dead, Samantha?*

"No, but I feel very...different."

Twitch, write. *You should feel different. We are all different.*

"But am I dead?" I asked. "And please don't say: 'Do you feel dead?'"

Your body went through a massive transformation, or metamorphosis, Samantha, but it did not die.

"Then why don't I breathe? Why can't I eat?"

That's one of the metamorphoses of which I speak. Or write. Your body, quite literally, is not the same, and thus does not have the same requirements.

"Like food or air."

Exactly. Yes.

"But I still need blood."

Of course. This is your new body's requirement.

"And so my new body is a killer, if it must feast on blood."

Does all blood need to come from that which is dead?

"No," I said, and my voice trailed off. I thought about something Kingsley had said earlier, about blood donors. Those who donated willingly...and those who most certainly did not. Blood debt perhaps.

Yes, Samantha, you are a far more powerful being than you were before, but what you make of your new physical form is up to you.

"I could choose to kill. Or not to kill."

Exactly. Yes. Just like everyone else.

"So I have a new body...but I still have the same moral code."

You are still you, sweet child, no matter what shape you take.

"Don't call me sweet child. It makes me want to cry."

Why?

"Because it sounds like you care about me. That you love me. But I don't know who you are or what you are."

Understood. But remember, all you have to do is ask.

"I have asked, but you've avoided the question."

I did not avoid. I simply gave you the answer you were ready for. Are you ready for the answer now?

I thought about that. I looked at my son sleeping on his back. My God, had the black halo actually grown in just a few minutes?

"Yes," I said.

We are many, Samantha. There are many of us here who have taken an active interest in you.

"So you are not Sephora?" A sense of alarm rang through me. Who was I talking to? Sephora had been the loving being I had spoken to in my last sessions.

She is here, of course, overseeing this dialogue. She is your personal guide, after all, who has been with you for all eternity.

"And who are you?"

With her blessing, I have come through.

"I don't understand."

I am a specialist in the arcane, Samantha.

"Arcane?"

In immortality. In the magicks of your realm, so to speak. Some would call them dark magicks, but they would be mistaken.

"Who are you?"

My hand paused, then wrote: *I am called by many names, through many lives, but I'm most commonly called Saint Germain.*

I'd heard of the name, of course. Saint Germain had been a European mystic. An alchemist of the highest order. He supposedly lived for centuries. And, from most accounts, never died. They say he ascended; that is, turned to light. A heavenly being who was just as comfortable in the spirit world as the physical world, often alternating between the two. And helping those in need. Immortal indeed.

And no, Samantha, I'm not a vampire, either.

"Then what are you?"

A seeker of truth.

"And did you find the truth?"

I found what I was looking for, yes. But there are always bigger questions, with bigger answers.

"So you eternally seek answers."

"Forever and ever."

"So why are you here with me now?"

You have called out for answers, Samantha Moon. I'm here to help you find them.

"But why you?"

Why not?

"Fine," I said and rubbed my head. I looked at my sick boy. "I want to talk about my son."

What would you like to know?

"Is he...is he going to die?"

There was a slight pause and the tingly sensation briefly abated, but then it returned. I realized that maybe I didn't want to know the answer. My hand moved across the page, and the gel ink flowed freely.

Your son has his own path, Samantha.

"What does that mean?"

We all follow our own paths, generally agreed on and known before our births.

"Who agrees on this?"

You. And many others.

"Which others?"

Those who care deeply about you. And those who care deeply about your son.

"And what's his path?" My voice was shaking now.

You know his path, Sam. You have foreseen it.

"Just tell me."

There was a short, agonizing pause, and then: *Your son's path will come to an end in this physical plane soon, as it has been decided upon, as he has decided, as well.*

"He's only a little boy, goddammit. What the hell does he know about anything?"

A little boy now, in the flesh, certainly. But a very wise old soul eternally.

I covered my eyes with my free hand. Tears poured between my fingers. It was all I could do to not throw the clipboard across the room.

"Why, why would he decide to end his life

now? Who would decide such a thing? Why take him from me?"

There are many, many reasons, Sam. And most of those involve the growth of his own soul, and the growth of the souls around him. Adapting to loss is a big step toward growth.

"It's a horrible, cruel step toward growth. How could you take my boy?"

I'm not taking him, Sam. No one can take. Leaving this world is his choice and his choice alone.

"But he's just a boy. He doesn't know what he's doing, and don't give me that crap that he's an old soul. He's not. He's just a little boy. A little, sick boy."

A little, sick boy with a highly evolved soul, Samantha. He understands his purpose here at the soul level, even if not at the physical level.

"Fuck you."

I'm sorry, Samantha.

I wept hard for a few minutes, barely able to control myself. Finally, when I could speak again, I said, "Are you there?"

Always.

"I have a question."

We are here for answers.

"Okay. Okay." I took a deep breath, and plunged forward. "Is there any way that I can save him?"

He does not need to be saved, Sam.

"Please."

We all have free will, Sam. You can do anything you want.

"So there is a way to save him?"

Of course there is. The body can heal itself immediately if it so chooses. What your doctors call miracles.

"The doctors are going down the wrong path," I said. "They think they're helping."

The doctors have diagnosed your son correctly, Samantha. There is nothing left for them to do. Although considerable, they have exhausted their collective expertise.

"But I know of another way."

I know, Sam. There are often many ways. The key is finding the one that feels the best.

"So my way is such a path."

Of course. But ask yourself: does it feel right?

"It feels right to me," I said quickly, although doubt ate at me.

Then so be it.

I took a deep breath. "Well, you haven't told me not to do it."

I would never tell you not to do anything, Samantha. This is called a free-will universe for a reason.

"But would you caution against it?"

I would caution against doing anything that doesn't feel right, Samantha. Always ask yourself if the choices you are doing feel right, and act according to your feelings. Then you will know you are on the right path. Always.

"But how do I know how I feel if I'm truly confused?"

You always know, Sam. Always.

Chapter Forty-six

I was driving.

My mind was still reeling from the phone call with Maddie. My mind was still reeling from my conversation with Kingsley. Reeling from my conversation with Saint Germain. Reeling from the possibility that my son could be saved. Possibly.

I was doing a lot of reeling and no doubt a lot of erratic driving, too. I forced myself to calm down. To focus.

It was early afternoon. My sister and daughter were with Anthony. I had work to do, and this was my time to do it, even if I was a royal mess.

I could head out to Simi Valley now, but I suspected I would be waiting a long, long time in the casino before anyone of note showed up. It was better to wait, and head out there later.

For now, I knew where to go. And it just so happened to be right around the corner, too.

***

I parked at the Wharton Museum and dashed across the parking lot, past the rich and not-so-famous dining at the Wharton outdoor cafe, and ducked into the main building, gasping for breath I didn't need, and feeling as if I had just run across hot coals.

"You okay?" asked the security guard at the door.

"I'm fine," I lied. Actually, I felt like shit.

He asked if I wanted some help and I waved him off and did my best to walk with some dignity toward the side offices, all too aware of a slight burning smell wafting up from my skin.

I've never felt sexier.

A few minutes later I was seated across from a shell-shocked Ms. Dickens. The old lady didn't look well, and I didn't blame her. A lot of bad luck had come her way. Granted, not as bad as the night guard I had found stuffed in an oversized Igloo.

"I guess the cat's out of the bag," she said. She was holding her forehead in her hands.

I nodded.

"No more hiding the fact that the sculpture was stolen."

"Sometimes there's more important things than stolen sculptures," I said. "Like dead people."

She looked up at me briefly, parting her hands slightly to do so. Her blank stare told me that perhaps she didn't subscribe to my philosophy. A stolen crystal egg, apparently, meant more to her than human life.

"Yes," she said, reluctantly agreeing. "I suppose so."

After a few more minutes of our strained silence, I asked her if I was still on the job. After all, part of my job description had been to help find the missing art piece before the official opening this weekend.

"Yes, of course," she snapped. "We still need to find it. We will just have to deal with the backlash of the theft and death. We've overcome tragedy before, and we will overcome this, too. The Wharton will be world famous someday. World famous. Mark my words."

I nearly stood up and cheered.

Now that we'd established that I still had a job, I thanked her for her time and left her at her desk, where she didn't move or acknowledge my departure.

The police had come and gone in the wee hours of the morning. With their initial investigation completed, the museum had opened on time and business was as usual. To a degree. The place was mostly empty; I felt as if I had it all to myself.

I headed deeper into the museum, looking for Mr. Wharton himself.

The resident ghost.

Chapter Forty-seven

I used my temporary security pass to enter the back room and although it was still daytime, you would never know it in here. The place was dark and ominous, and knowing there was a ghost creeping around here made the fine hair at the back of my neck stand on end.

There were two security cameras back here, both placed in such a way that they could see anyone coming and going. The cameras could also see down the main aisle that led between all the side aisles.

Except the cameras weren't working for 20 minutes. Long enough for someone to come in and get out with a prized sculpture worth hundreds of thousands of dollars, or whatever he could get for it on eBay. Long enough to kill a guard and stuff him in a freezer.

As I stood there taking in the back room, I

heard shuffling down a side aisle. A ghost? A murderer? Neither. A few seconds later, a young girl emerged. She looked thoroughly freaked out. I didn't blame her. A theft, a murder, a ghost and a vampire. Had I been anyone but me, I might have been freaked, too.

She saw me and gasped, clutching her throat. I smiled apologetically and she relaxed a little. She was holding a box of something. Small museum pieces, although I couldn't see what. She moved quickly past me with a forced smile, and left by the same door I had just stepped through.

Crime scenes can take hours or weeks to clear. The fact that the Santa Ana Police Department had cleared this one in a matter of hours was telling: it meant there was little, if any, evidence. The crime scene itself had been trampled to hell. If there had been evidence, it was probably gone.

With very few clues to collect, and with little hope of collecting anything of value, the museum had been given the green light to open for business with no apparent disruptions. That didn't mean the Santa Ana PD would take the murder case any less seriously. It just meant they had little to work with.

Although not on public display, many of the artifacts back here were still highly valuable and some were one-of-a-kind. The muted, indirect lighting was no doubt UV and IR free so as not to cause any damage to the highly sensitive paintings and sculptures and various rare artifacts.

The lighting could be adjusted, I could see. The

young lady had had it as high as it would go. Again, I didn't blame her. I reached over and turned it down low. No doubt Eddie—if Eddie was indeed watching me back in the control room—wondered why the hell I had done that. I wondered if he would believe me if I told him that it was to better see the ghost of Mr. Wharton.

Now with the room mostly in deep shadows, my senses sprang to life. Granted, it was still daytime, and I wouldn't be fully alive and alert until the sun set, but the cool darkness in the back room was the next best thing and I was feeling a little better.

I headed deeper into the room. The air around me was electrified. Little squigglies of light danced before my eyes. These supercharged particles emanated a glow that only I could see and it gave the room added light. At least for me.

All of my senses told me that I was alone in the back room. I walked slowly down the center aisle. I felt my mind reaching out before me, searching for something both physical and non-physical.

I was getting a lot of feedback. I sensed strange energy around a lot of the artifacts, for instance. Some of these relics had been acquired over the years—not necessarily by the museum, but by others—through force or coercion. These artifacts had a lot of negative energy around them, a darkness that surrounded them. Cursed, perhaps. Other artifacts and pieces of art had a lot of bright energy buzzing around them, light particles that swarmed like bees around a beehive, and I realized these were aspects of the owners' souls still attached to the artifacts. Perhaps forever attached.

Owner and art forever linked.

These were strange concepts that I was only now beginning to understand through my own strange second sight.

I soon found myself standing in the very aisle where the freezer box was located. There was still yellow police 'caution tape' around it. Although the police had gathered all the evidence they could early this morning, they could—and probably would—come back for a follow-up investigation, with the hope of acquiring additional evidence. Of course, the tape itself meant little to someone determined to tamper with the evidence. I wasn't going to tamper with the evidence.

Instead, I just stood there, getting a feel for the place. A man had died here not too long ago and I idly wondered where his spirit had gone. Was he still here, roaming the museum with Mr. Wharton?

I didn't know, but there was some strange energy around the ice box, and it very well could have been his spirit, but the energy was scattered and without much shape. I suspected the murdered security guard had gone on to wherever most spirits go on to.

It was then that I knew I was being watched, and not just by Eddie in the control room. Something had appeared behind me. Something that caused the hair on my neck to stand up.

I turned and was not very surprised to see a figure taking shape behind me. A human-shaped nexus gathered the surrounding light particles the way a black hole attracts all the heavenly bodies around it. Unlike a black hole, these light particles didn't disappear into a dimension occupied by only Charlie Sheen and Mel Gibson. These light particles formed a shape I readily recognized.

Mr. Bernard Wharton.

And when the last of the particles morphed into the shape of a fedora sitting slightly askew on its head, the entity before me nodded. I did the only thing I could think of and nodded back. In the control room, Eddie was getting quite a show. What Eddie made of the show, I didn't know or care.

And because I knew there wasn't any sound being recorded, I felt free to speak. "You know who killed the guard, don't you, Mr. Wharton?"

The figure before me didn't react at first, but then finally nodded, almost reluctantly.

I was about to ask the rather pointed question of *who* had killed the guard, but now the ghost was moving, flitting down the hallway and into another, darker room. I assumed I was meant to follow him and so I did—into the same dark room.

I didn't bother with the lights. I could see that we were in the shipping and receiving room. I knew this because there was a huge plastic bag filled with Styrofoam popcorn hovering over one of the tables, the *shipping* table, I presumed. There were computers, and crates and other random knickknacks.

The room obviously doubled as a sort of storage room, too, with brooms and mops and cleaning supplies propped near the door.

Mr. Wharton led me deeper into the room to a work station off in the far corner. Random boxes were piled here, most of them opened and discarded. There were also packing supplies here and other boxes that appeared ready to be shipped.

He floated over to one of the boxes. I followed behind and looked down. The box was packed and taped, but the recipient hadn't yet been filled out. Correction, there was a single letter on the box, an "M", followed by a squiggly line, as if the writer had lost heart.

Or been scared to death.

Mr. Wharton stood next to me. Some of his crackling energy reached out to me, attaching itself to me, and as it did so, something very strange started to happen.

Flashing images appeared in my thoughts. Images I had never seen before. Images that weren't mine. Memories that weren't mine

They were *his* images. *His* memories. Mr. Wharton's.

I saw a flash of a security guard wearing gloves and working on an electrical panel. Perhaps the panel that powered the security cameras. I recognized the guard easily enough, especially since I had found him dead in the cold storage box.

The next flash. Now the guard was standing over this very box, writing something, when his head suddenly snapped around, eyes thoroughly spooked.

The next image was the same guard heading through the back room. He was following me, but he wasn't really following me. He was following Mr. Wharton. And for good reason.

Every now and then Mr. Wharton would knock something over, and each sound would cause the guard to jump...and consequently to investigate further. Deeper into the bowels of the back room.

Toward, I saw, the cold storage freezer.

Something else fell over—a marble Buddha, I think—and the guard nearly jumped out of his skin. But he continued on, doggedly, perhaps driven by fascination, or perhaps driven by the sick realization that tonight wasn't going according to plan. That someone was watching him. That someone knew what he was up to. Perhaps at any other time he would have turned away in fear. But not tonight. No, tonight—or rather, the night in question—he continued forward, inevitably, toward Mr. Wharton and the ice box.

Thad the security guard paused when he heard another noise. A noise that came from the ice box itself. A thumping, knocking sound. I even had a brief, flashing image of Mr. Wharton reaching down *through* the box and rapping something inside.

Thad the security guard whined a little. He was also making small, gasping sounds.

From a perspective from somewhere near the

ice box, I watched—or, more accurately, Mr. Wharton watched—as the terrified man reached down and slowly opened the ice chest.

I could see that Thad didn't really want to open it, that he was scared shitless. But he seemed somehow *compelled* to open it. Like a man possessed. Which got me thinking.

Either way, as the lid came up, all hell broke loose.

The images jumped crazily. No, it wasn't the image that jumped crazily. It was Mr. Wharton moving rapidly. One moment he was down by the ice chest, and the next he was hovering somewhere above the security guard. The ice box was open. Frost and mist issued out, swirling around the man.

Mr. Wharton's attention shifted, and since I was seeing this through his eyes, his memory, my attention shifted, too.

To a shelf above the refrigerated box.

On the shelf, marked very neatly, were rows of stone tools and weapons; in particular, stone hatchets.

An arm reached up for the hatchet, and I was startled to see that it was Mr. Wharton's arm. A very real-looking arm. But not entirely real. Although solid-looking, I could still see through it.

Ectoplasm. A ghost body.

Now that very real-looking arm, draped in a slightly dusty reddish dinner jacket, removed the hatchet from the shelf. No doubt this was a Native American hatchet, or another tribal weapon from somewhere around the world. My knowledge of such artifacts was slim to none.

But one thing was obvious: it was heavy-looking, and it was topped by a razor-sharp flint head. A weapon used, no doubt, in battle or for skinning animals.

Or, in this case, for murder.

Thad must have heard something. As he turned to look, crying out, the hatchet flashed down and buried deep into his forehead. Thad jerked and nearly bit off his tongue. His left eye popped clean out of his head, to dangle by its neon-red optical nerves. I next watched in sick fascination as Mr. Wharton worked the hatchet free from the dead man's skull. When he did, Thad the security guard toppled into the freezer.

The ghost of Mr. Wharton calmly shut the lid, returned the bloody hatchet to its proper place, and promptly disappeared.

Chapter Forty-eight

I was at Heroes, where only one person knew my name, and that was just the way I liked it.

I had already picked up Tammy from school and dropped her off at my sister's. Danny, remarkably, was with Anthony at the hospital. My sister had asked if I would be there as well, and I said I would as soon as I could. She didn't like it but knew that only something very, very important would keep me away from my son.

Now, it was almost five and it had been a helluva day. Soon I would be heading out to Simi Valley, but first I needed to speak with Fang, my rock. And since our relationship had graduated to the physical level, I paid him a visit before heading out. The bar was mostly empty and we could speak freely enough. I caught him up to date on the past few days' activities.

"So the crystal egg was in the box," said Fang.

He wasn't polishing the stereotypical glass; instead, he was cutting lime wedges.

"Yup."

"Any idea where he was going to send it?"

"Hard to say with only an 'M' in the address. Could have been his grandma. A P.O. Box anywhere. And before you ask, his name was Thad."

"Thad?"

"Yup."

"Is that a real name?"

"As real as Fang."

He grinned. "Pretty clever idea just shipping that sucker out right under their noses."

"Would have worked, too, if Mr. Wharton hadn't cleaved his skull nearly in two."

"With a five hundred year old war ax. Very fitting, being that this was his museum and all."

"And that he protects to this day," I said.

Fang leaned across the bar. As he did so, his two canine teeth clacked together like two marbles. He said, "So did you unpack the box right there?"

"No. I left it for Ms. Dickens. She opened it with a few other staff members standing nearby... and when she did, well, she nearly wept."

"A murder is one thing, but the theft of a piece of art is another."

"It is to a small museum trying to make a name for itself."

"Our world is weird," said Fang.

"Tell me about it."

His eyes crinkled a little. Maybe he got some squirting lime juice in them. "How did you explain that you knew the egg was in the box?"

"I told her I had a hunch."

"Your hunches are pretty damn good."

"Better than most," I said.

He nodded. "So the ghost of Mr. Wharton killed the security guard."

"He wasn't going to let anyone steal from his museum."

"Death by ghost," said Fang.

"Our world is weird," I said, and both Fang and I smiled at each other.

"So, it will go down as an unsolved crime?"

"No doubt," I said.

"Would be hard to arrest Mr. Wharton," he said, laughing lightly. He added, "Can a ghost still go to hell for killing?"

"You'll have to ask God."

He grinned again, and his eyes did this sort of sparkly thing that made my heart beat a little faster. Knowing my thoughts, he smiled brightly.

"Oh, give it a rest," I said. "You have a nice smile, so what?"

"Whatever you say, Moon Dance." He reached out and took my hands. "Have you thought about my request?"

"Not really, no. Too much on my mind."

He nodded. "I understand. Things have been crazy."

He squeezed my hands a little tighter. His

hands were soft in spots, but rough in others. They were the hands of a man who poured drinks for a living, but worked on muscle cars when he could. They were also the hands of a man who had killed three people.

"I regret the killings," said Fang, squeezing my hands a little tighter and reading my thoughts. "I'm not a killer, Sam."

"Then why do you want to be a vampire?"

"Because I want to be with you," he said, bringing my knuckles to his lips and kissing them lightly. "Forever."

Chapter Forty-nine

The traffic out to Simi Valley was so bad that I was tempted to just pull over and take flight.

I resisted and two hours later, after winding my way through the foothills that connect Northridge to Simi Valley, I headed down a long incline toward the glittering lights that porn built.

Porn Valley. Or, as some people call it, Sili*cone* Valley.

As a one-time federal agent, I knew that nearly 90% of all legally produced pornographic films made in the United States were produced in studios based in the San Fernando Valley, of which Simi Valley was the heart.

The key phrase here was "legally produced." Other porn was produced here, as well. Some not so legal.

This, of course, was what made me nervous.

My cell rang. It was Danny. Oh, joy. Then

again, he might have news about my son. Ever the cautious driver, I hooked my Bluetooth around my ear and clicked on.

"Hey, Sam," he said. His voice sounded strained. Something was either obstructing his throat or he had been crying. Or was still crying.

Shit. "Hey."

"He's dying, isn't he?" But Danny didn't really get the words out. Not really. Instead, a choked, strangled sound came out, and it was a horrible sound to hear. "Please, tell me the truth, Sam. Please. I'm so scared."

I closed my eyes. His pain went straight to my heart. I debated how much to tell him, until I realized he had a right to know.

"Yes, he is," I said.

Danny wept harder than I had ever heard him weep, harder than I had ever heard any man weep, and we cried together on the phone for many, many miles.

***

A trail of red brake lights snaked ahead of me as far as the eye could see. Although an hour outside of L.A., traffic in Southern California knew no city boundaries.

When I had hung up with Danny, I was an emotional wreck. Still driving, I did my best to compose myself, wiping the tears from my cheeks. Say what you want about the guy, the man loved his kids.

Traffic picked up, and as I worked my way into Simi Valley, one building clearly shone brighter than all others, up on a large hill—or a mountain, as one little girl put it—the Ronald Reagan Museum.

Below it, near the base and about three miles south of me, glittering in a far different way, was a massive casino. The Juarez Indian Tribe, on land reserved for them, had built one of the most popular casinos in Southern California, and even from here, as I made my way off the freeway, the casino lights flashed and strobed and practically jiggled—anything to lure dollars away from wallets.

A few minutes later, with the half moon hanging high in the sky, I pulled up to the casino and stepped out of my minivan. I scanned the fifteen-story facade of the hotel. Some of the windows were bright, but most were dark.

Maddie's words came flooding back to me. Perhaps they had been unlocked because I was staring up at the massive hotel, or perhaps I had gotten a psychic hit. Sometimes I didn't know. Hey, I'm still figuring this stuff out as I go.

Either way, I heard her words again: "We take the vader up."

The vader.

The elevator.

Maddie was here, in this hotel. Somewhere.

I was sure of it.

<u>Chapter Fifty</u>

I was dressed to kill. Or at least to seriously maim someone. I was wearing a tight black dress, fully aware of my rounded hips and thighs on the one hand, but not giving a shit on the other. It had been a while since I had worn this black dress and I had forgotten how much skin it showed.

How much *pale* skin, that is.

I'm a jeans-and-tee-shirt kind of gal, but sometimes you have to look the part. And what was the part I was looking? I didn't know, but dressing as a slutty whore in a casino in Porn Valley seemed the best way to blend in.

The black man in the photographs was named Carl Luck. A known drug dealer and pornographer. And, apparently, murderer and kidnapper.

Allegedly, of course.

I parked my minivan in the back of the crowded parking lot. After huffing it across the vast lot, I strode past an epic water fountain with a stone eagle feather motif. I walked under a glittering eagle feather arch, and across an eagle feather tiled mosaic near the entry way.

I sensed a pattern here.

Inside, the Moon Feather Casino was epic. I felt lost just standing there at the entrance. Where to start? I had no clue. I had Carl Luck's face seared, as they say, on the back of my retina. I would know the guy anywhere. Now it was just a matter of finding him without attracting attention to myself, or getting myself kicked out by the tribal police.

If I were a regular, where would I go in a casino?

I had no clue. I would have thought the bar, except the whole damn place was one big, honking bar. Waitresses crisscrossed everywhere, each carrying trays of colorful drinks. The waitresses were all middle-aged and tired-looking. They wore shiny leotards that showed a lot of stockinged legs. An eagle tail feather hung behind them, seemingly flapping as they walked.

Oh, brother.

Ignoring the occasionally discreet and mostly not-so-discreet stares of men old enough to be my grandfather, I made a circuit of the casino. At least, I think I did. Quite frankly, I had no clue where I ended up at. It all looked the same. Exits everywhere. Restaurants everywhere. Hallways to exotic-sounding clubs. And the games. My God, the games. Rows upon rows of video poker and slot machines, with every conceivable theme. There were elaborate and colorful ancient Egyptian-themed slots: "Play with the Pharaohs!" Rows of ancient Mayan slot machines with pictures of treasures and stepped pyramids. An ancient Troy slot machine with a flashing Trojan horse, but instead of men pouring out of its underbelly, golden coins poured free. Hell, I could receive a thumbnail history lesson all while losing my money. If anything, the casino was a "Who's Who" of the ancient world.

And as I walked past a row of Easter Island slot machines, complete with megalithic-shaped heads, I decided to wait it out at what appeared to be the casino's central bar.

I ordered a house white wine and noted idly that the bartender wasn't anywhere near as cute as Fang. And as I sat there, drinking it sporadically and watching the crowd, I realized that this was a little like looking for a needle in a haystack.

That is, if the needle was a child-trafficking killer.

So I decided to pull out the big guns.

Chapter Fifty-one

I closed my eyes and did my best to clear my thoughts.

It's hard to clear your thoughts with the sounds of a casino assaulting your ears. Maybe that's the casino's secret plan. Assault the senses. Overstimulate them, confuse them, and thus lead you down dark roads where pulling out gobs of money and shoving them into a machine for "credits" suddenly seems like a damn good idea.

Or maybe the machines were just fucking annoying.

Anyway, I closed my eyes and cleared my thoughts and ignored the guy who just sat next to me, reeking of alcohol and cigarettes. I tried to home in on my guy.

I let a single name ease into my thoughts:

Carl Luck.

I let his image slide in next. The picture of him

exiting McDonald's, with little Maddie and her mom, Lauren, in tow. In the picture he's looking down, perhaps at Maddie. But it's a good shot of his face. His strong cheek bones. His flat forehead. The tight position of his eyes in relation to his nose. All of this was permanently emblazoned in my thoughts.

Next, I did something that was new even to me, and it just sort of happened on its own. In my mind's eye, I saw my thoughts rippling away from me, further and further out like a widening gyre. And as my mind reached out, it seemed to touch down on everyone around me, searching.

Searching.

It kept reaching out, kept searching—

"Excuse me, baby?"

My probing thoughts came racing back, nearly slamming physically back into me. Jolting me. I gasped. It took me a moment to orient myself, and when I did, my smiling drunk neighbor's face was about three inches from my own. Three purple, wormy veins snaked just under the skin of his bulbous nose.

"What?" I asked, confused. I was still coming back. Back into my body. I had been out there somehow. Out in the casino. Somehow out of my body.

Sweet Jesus.

"Hey, baby, *you* were the one talking to *me*."

"I wasn't talking to you."

"Sure, baby. You kept saying something about

luck. And, since I'm the only lucky bastard sitting next to you, I figured you were talking to me."

"I wasn't talking to you, sorry."

He put a firm hand on my bare thigh. "Of course you were, angel. Tonight's my lucky night."

He was a big guy. Granted, when you're five foot three, even sixth graders look big. But this guy was closing in on three hundred, and nearly had me by three times my own weight. I've got nothing against big guys. Actually, I find them adorable. But not drunk guys who lay their drunken fat hands on my thighs.

I put my hand on his and he smiled. This was encouraging for him. And, apparently, some drunken guy green light. He immediately tried to move his hand up the inside of my thigh. Except his hand didn't move. I calmly lifted it off my thigh and started squeezing.

"Hey!"

"Go away."

"My hand!"

"Go far away."

I let go and he tumbled backwards off the stool, his feet flying up. He landed with a squishy thud. Keys and a cell phone toppled out of his pockets. Along with a condom. Eww. The not-quite-as-good-looking-as-Fang bartender rushed over to us, but I only shrugged and made a drinking motion. The guy got to his feet, gathered his stuff, and hurried away from me without looking back.

The bartender lingered briefly, certain that

something strange had gone on, but then moved further down the bar to take an order, glancing at me a final time.

Way to stay inconspicuous, Sam. Easy, girl.

With the excitement over and alone once again, I closed my eyes and went through the previous steps and cast my thoughts outward.

And they continued outward until they reached the far end of the casino. I went through a double door and into an exclusive poker room. And sitting near the poker table was a dead ringer for public enemy #1, Mr. Carl Luck.

Whose luck might have just run out.

Hey, I had to say it.

As an experiment, I cast my thoughts even further out, up through the hotel, floor after floor, but there seemed to be a limit to this. The further I got, the more scattered my thoughts were.

I retracted them, this time not so violently, and opened my eyes. When I had steadied myself, I plunked down a $10 bill, got up, and headed for the far side of the casino.

To the poker room.

Chapter Fifty-two

Feeling as if I had done this before, I wove my way past roulette tables and blackjack tables, and past tables of made-up games I had never heard before. Games like Flash Poker and Three-Card Texas Slam.

Okay, now they're just making stuff up.

As I walked, I was aware that a lot of flesh was showing and a part of me didn't entirely mind. A steady diet of blood, staying out of the sun, and my own nighttime jogs had done wonders for my body. The ultimate Atkins Diet. I was still naturally curvy, but a petite curvy. Petite and now roped with muscle.

Some men looked. Some women did, too. I wasn't the sexiest or prettiest woman here, not by a long shot, but I suspected I projected a certain presence. What that presence was, I didn't know. Confidence? Blood lust?

Soon, I reached the far corner of the casino, where I wasn't too surprised to see the same double doors there. There were two guys—both Native American—standing just outside the open doors, and I suspected they would have stopped most people. But I put on my best "don't fuck with me" look and they simply blinked and smiled and let me through.

And as I swept through, I wondered: Had they let me in because of my "don't fuck with me look" or something else?

What that something was, I didn't know. But the words "mind control" came to mind.

Too weird.

I surveyed the room. Definitely high rollers. Seven men were seated around the table, no women. Two of the men were wearing Arab *keffiyehs*. Another was wearing a white cowboy hat, and the remaining four were a mix of ethnicities. All were dressed immaculately. None noticed me. All were intent on the dealer who was currently shuffling. A few more security types stood around the room, all of them Native American. The casino's own security, no doubt. There were a handful of plush chairs surrounding the main poker table, and these were filled with babes. Various hookers, no doubt. And at a private bar on the far side of the room sat Carl Luck, wearing shades and drinking a draft beer. He was watching the game intently.

My heart slammed against a rib or two. My first instinct was to fly across the room and slam his face into the bar, and keep slamming it until he told me where Maddie was.

Calm down. Deep breaths.

Instead, I crossed the big room as calmly as I could and found a stool next to Carl Luck.

***

He was a big man. Not as big as some of the other men in my life, but he was certainly up there. Other than glancing at me from over his shades, Carl did little to acknowledge me. The thick black man smelled of nice cologne. His shiny, mottled boots were ostrich skin. His maroon leather jacket fit him perfectly. If I had to guess, I would say Carl Luck had recently come into a lot of money. The man in the picture at McDonald's had been nowhere near as slick.

"Who's winning?" I asked innocently.

Carl slowly turned his shiny head. Nothing else moved. He was leaning one elbow on the counter. His elbow looked exceptionally sharp. His eyes were hidden behind the cool shades.

"Captain Jack's up," he said. His deep-throated voice was as smooth as smooth gets. He sounded like a radio talk show host. The kind women swoon for.

"Always better to be up than down, I say." Except I didn't know what the hell I was talking about.

Carl looked at me but said nothing, although I

could hear his nasally breathing from here. One of his nostrils was backed up.

Gee, I wonder why.

"Who's Captain Jack?" I asked.

"Cowboy hat."

"Of course. Should have figured that one out."

Carl turned back to the game. Once again, only his head moved. Nothing else. Correction. His jaw tightened a little. I was making him nervous.

He's wondering who the hell I am.

Good question. This was an exclusive, high-stakes room that I really had no business being in—and no real reason for being here.

Other than to find Maddie.

Someone from the table whooped loudly. Captain Jack. He yanked off his hat and waved it like a cowboy riding a bucking bronco. A whole mass of chips just got pushed his way. He whooped again.

Next to me, Carl grinned slightly.

He's with Captain Jack, I thought.

One white and one black, said little Maddie.

"Do you play?" I asked.

"Hell no."

"Why not?"

"It's a two hundred and fifty thou buy-in."

"More than my house."

"More than most houses."

"I bet they fly these guys in," I said. "I heard some hotels do that."

"Shit. They roll out the red carpet for these

brothers. Fly them in, bring them women, and anything else they want."

"What else could they want?"

"Anything."

I nodded. Carl was tense. Very tense. The cords along his neck were throbbing. His hands opened and closed. Waves of apprehension emanated from him.

I said, "Free hotel room. Free everything, I bet."

"Yeah, something like that," he said. He turned his back to me.

So Carl and Captain Jack were staying here. And now Carl was shutting down and I didn't want to push it.

"Well, the nickel slot machines are calling my name," I said.

But Carl didn't acknowledge me as I left, although I could feel his eyes on me as I crossed the room and exited through the double doors.

Chapter Fifty-three

I leaned a shoulder against a smooth wall and exhaled a billowing plume of gray smoke. I was standing just inside a narrow hallway that led to the casino's bathrooms and public phones. From here, I had a good view of the double doors of the exclusive parlor.

I inhaled deeply, filling my lungs to the maximum. Smoking did nothing for me. No smoker's high. Nothing. No nicotine addiction. Nothing. For me, smoking was a purely voluntary act. It was one of the few things that I could do without a violent reaction. So I did it because I could.

The good thing about casinos is that you can smoke in them. The good thing about being a vampire is that you don't get lung cancer.

At least, that's what they tell me. And by *they*,

I mean Fang. The man was my sole source for all things vampiric.

I found myself grinning thinking about the Toothless Wonder. Toothless because his canines had been removed. His dogteeth, as they are sometimes called.

His *vampire* teeth.

Interesting thing about that, since my own teeth had never once changed size or shape in the six years since I'd been unwillingly recruited into the creature of the night club. Admittedly, it made sense that longer canine teeth would aid a vampire. Of course, so would a hypodermic needle. Longer teeth aided creatures who hunted with their mouth, those who didn't have the benefit of hands or weapons. Longer teeth latched onto prey, held it down. Longer teeth aided in tearing into the flesh.

I couldn't eat flesh. I needed only a steady flow of blood to be sustained. I didn't need to kill other creatures, either.

A voluntary source would be adequate.

A donor.

These thoughts were new to me. They were revolutionary. They made me look at myself differently.

I didn't have to kill.

I only had to drink.

Of course, I received my supply of blood from a local butchery, so I didn't kill. But the blood was also disgusting and mixed with hundreds of other creatures, some of which might very well be diseased or sick.

All mixed in a big bloody soup for yours truly to enjoy night after night.

But it didn't have to be that way, did it? All I needed was a steady source.

I thought of Fang. I also thought of his request.

Make me a vampire.

I inhaled again, squinting through the smoke even though it didn't really hurt my eyes. The room beyond the double doors was still quiet. A few people passed in and out, but not Carl Luck or Captain Jack.

Jesus, had Fang proposed to me tonight? I mean, he had taken my hand and said he wanted to be with me for all eternity.

A proposal if I'd ever heard one.

Wow.

I dashed out my cigarette in a glass ash tray around the corner, then went back to my post just inside the hallway. I would think about Fang's proposal later. At the moment, Fang's proposal was way down on my list.

High on my list was the grim realization that I was certain—dead certain—that I was going to kill two men tonight.

Thirty minutes later, a group of wealthy men emerged from the parlor room. Only one looked particularly cheerful, a tall man wearing a *keffiyeh*. Captain Jack, who followed behind, looked like he was in a sour mood.

Carl Luck slapped him on his back

reassuringly, and the two men headed off toward a bank of elevators.

Vaders.

Chapter Fifty-four

Fifteen minutes later, I took the elevator up to the upper suites.

The luxury suites. The high rollers suites. Suites where the big boys stayed with their big bucks. Suites that were spacious enough that you probably couldn't hear someone scream. Especially a little girl.

I set my jaw as the elevator doors opened. My purse was still over my shoulder. Cool air met me in the spacious hallway. I could turn right or left. I automatically turned right, feeling my way.

The hallway was lined with polished tables and flowers. I doubted the other floors had polished tables and flowers. The doors here were recessed deep in the walls and inlaid with brass relief designs. The designs were, you guessed it, eagle feathers. The doors, I saw, were also designed for security. Although the reliefs were in brass, the doors themselves were made of steel.

I continued down the hall, guided entirely by my sixth sense. As I made a right turn, a small buzzing began just inside my eardrum. And the further I walked down the hallway, the louder the buzzing became.

I found myself staring at one recessed doorway in particular. It was on my left and it looked like all the others.

Except it didn't *feel* like all the others. I was drawn to it, and even as I was drawn to it, my innate warning system—the buzzing in my ears—grew louder and louder.

There's danger here.

The gilded door gleamed dully in the muted lights. I was alone in the hallway. I couldn't hear a sound, and my hearing was damn good.

Still, my head buzzed; my skin prickled.

Behind this door was a terrified little girl—the same little girl who had been calling me these past few days.

The steel door might as well have been a vault door. The hotel gave its exalted guests a lot of security and privacy.

Too much privacy.

The door would have multiple locks, including a deadbolt and no doubt another one elsewhere. Maybe near the floor or ceiling. This wasn't your standard hotel door. Up here, on this floor, nothing was standard.

Sometimes I wondered how strong I really was.

It's not an easy thing to test, unless you want to draw attention to yourself. A few years back, while out jogging, I paused next to an old Volkswagen Beetle. On a whim, I reached down, felt underneath, and then lifted it three feet off the ground.

A few weeks ago I had punched through a bulletproof prison glass and nearly killed a man.

A steel, ornamental, security door seemed forbidding in and of itself. I could have knocked, sure. I could have called the police and pleaded my case. With luck, an emergency search warrant might be issued.

Think again, Sam. This is reservation land. Things are done differently here.

How differently, I didn't know, but I suspected the hotel would think twice, or maybe even three or four times, before upsetting a guest who plunks down $250K on a card game...and then loses.

Yes, I could have done a lot of things differently at this moment, but none of them felt right.

None, that is, except this.

I raised my foot, leaned back, and drove the heel of my foot as hard as I could into the door. Obliterating my expensive high heel, and obliterating the door hinges, too.

The steel slab fell inward, landing with a thunderous crash.

Chapter Fifty-five

I instinctively stood to one side of the doorway. The metallic echo of the falling door continued to reverberate throughout the suite.

Hell of an entrance.

But there was no one directly in front of me, and as I slipped inside, kicking off my worthless high heels, the alarm in my head continued to buzz, stronger than ever.

Something was very, very wrong. More wrong than I had previously imagined. What it was, I didn't know. Yet.

Maybe I should have called the police. Or at least had a gun.

The suite was opulent. Sickeningly so. No doubt it costs thousands a night, although a guy like Captain Jack probably had it comped.

I'd never had anything comped in my life.

The balcony doors were wide open. Even from

the doorway, I had a majestic view of the sweeping southern hillside...and the Ronald Reagan Library.

I had the right place.

Where the door had fallen, it had shattered about a dozen expensive Italian marble slabs. I stepped over the fallen door, crunched over the broken tile, and slipped deeper into the room.

***

The suite was designed with two main wings that branched off from the main living room. The hallway to my left led to the back rooms, and a shorter hallway to the right led off to a kitchen space and a billiard room and bar. The bar was big enough to liquor up the entire casino.

So far, I hadn't seen anyone. Or heard anyone.

But they were here.

I knew it.

Standing just outside the hallway to the bedroom wing, I closed my eyes and searched for them. Or at least tried to. My senses were chaotic, unclear. I needed a clear head to focus, and focusing now was nearly impossible.

They're in the bedrooms. One of the bedrooms.

I turned down the hallway wing, padding softly over the smooth tiles with my bare feet. There were four doors along this hallway, two on each side. This luxury suite was bigger than three of my houses put together.

They knew I was here. They had to have

known. No way that fallen door went undetected. The alarm inside my head continued to sound, a buzzing that surrounded my head like so many wasps.

The doors into the bedrooms were all double doors. Three of the four double doors stood open. The doors at the far end of the hallway were the only ones closed.

They're in there. Doing whatever it is that they're doing.

I felt sick, but I continued forward. I paused at each open door, but the rooms, although packed with luggage, were empty.

Now standing at the far door at the far end of the hallway, I heard a little voice whimpering.

Ah, fuck.

I tried the handle. It was unlocked.

I inhaled deeply, took hold of the handle, and threw the door open.

I thought I was ready for anything.

But I wasn't ready for this.

Chapter Fifty-six

The first thing I saw was a table. A medical table of some type. It was sitting in the center of the spacious room.

The next thing I saw was a little girl on the table.

Maddie.

Oh, sweet Jesus.

She was dead, or close to it.

Red tubes ran from her arms to plastic bags full of blood. Her blood. She was wrapped in a white robe covered with droplets of blood. Her blood. Her eyes were closed and now I could just make out her little chest rising and falling slowly. A single light shone down on her.

What the fuck was going on?

My first instinct was to run to her. But I resisted. My agency training superseded my natural instinct.

She's breathing; she's not dead; stay still.

I knew I wasn't alone. Other than Maddie, I knew someone else was in the room.

Perhaps more than one.

Psychic hits are great. But they only get you so far.

At the open doorway, I paused, listening. I heard nothing. No, wait. I heard breathing from deeper inside the room. Nasally breathing.

Mr. Carl Luck.

So where was Captain Jack?

He's in here, too. The sick bastard is in here, too. Siphoning Maddie's blood.

For what?

The answer was all too obvious.

He's a vampire.

"You got that right, little lady."

I couldn't pinpoint the location of the voice, but it seemed to come from somewhere above. I was also all too aware that the speaker had read my thoughts.

"Right again, little lady. Now don't be shy, step on in here. We don't bite." The voice chuckled.

My head was buzzing. Danger was everywhere. Perhaps at every turn. I looked down the hall. There was nothing. The danger was all in this room.

I had seen only one other vampire in my life, and that was just the other day. The vampire who had attacked me years ago had done so in a blur.

For the first time in a long, long time, I didn't know what to do.

Meanwhile, there was a little girl bleeding to death.

I hadn't used a gun in a long time, but I wished I had one now. Carl I wasn't worried about. Captain Jack was another story. Captain Jack was the enigma. The kink in the chain.

Maddie made a small, mewing sound. I saw something forming around her. A black halo.

Shit.

I considered dashing in and grabbing her, but I knew a recently fed vampire like Captain Jack would be powerful. Not to mention I knew instinctively that Carl Luck was armed...and not with just a traditional weapon, either.

It was the reason my alarm was sounding off so loudly.

He had silver bullets in his gun. I was sure of it.

The moment I thought that, the southern voice laughed heartily from somewhere in the room.

The black halo around Maddie continued growing.

I didn't know what to do.

It was an ambush, that much was for sure.

And that's when I heard a noise from behind me. When I turned to look, I saw a sight that was both welcomed and very, very surreal.

It was Aaron King, the old detective from Los Angeles, slipping into the hallway behind me. He raised a finger to his lips to shush me. I nodded.

Maddie needed to be saved.

Now.

I dashed into the room, trusting my instincts, trusting Aaron King, and praying like hell we all made it through this alive.

Chapter Fifty-seven

I had a hard time zeroing in on the vampire, but I knew, could *feel*, exactly where Carl Luck was in the room.

The heavy-set drug dealer—and apparent *blood* dealer—was crouching in the far corner of the huge bedroom, taking aim. I twisted my body just as a shot rang out. The bullet grazed my shoulder, searing it, and impacted the wall behind me.

I crouched and ran forward, sprinting as fast as I could. The room blurred past me.

Another shot rang out. But I was going too fast to turn or duck or do anything. A wicked pain kicked me in the stomach. But I didn't stop running, and now I was leaping.

Carl Luck screamed and shrank back, and I drove my flattened hand, with its sharp, pointed nails, straight through his throat. Through skin and Adam's apple, and through his spine, as well, severing it.

He jerked hard and instantly shit his pants.

Blood spurted everywhere as I pulled my hand free. I was already spinning, searching for the vampire, but there was no one there.

The pain in my stomach flared mightily, and I nearly doubled over. I gasped, fought to stay on my feet. It had been a silver bullet, I was sure of it. The pain...nearly unbearable. The searing pain...so similar to the crossbow bolt of a few months ago. Had the bullet gone all the way through? I didn't know.

Something flashed overhead. A white blur.

I looked up, raising my hand, just as something dropped down from above. A wide fist, like a hammer, that drove my head straight down into the floor.

The force of the blow was unlike anything I had ever felt before. How it didn't kill me, I don't know.

I lay there, gasping, struggling for breath, bleeding on the floor from my stomach, shoulder and mouth. My nose was broken, I was sure of it. Perhaps my jaw, too. The force of the punch had driven my face into the tiles, cracking the tiles. Blood flowed freely, filling the cracks like little crimson tributaries.

Someone grabbed my hair, lifted me up. My jaw hung slack. Yeah, it was broken. Shattered, perhaps.

"So who do we have here?" I heard a voice ask

from somewhere seemingly far away. It was the same voice I had heard earlier from the hallway. The same southern drawl.

He continued lifting until I was facing him. It was Captain Jack, of course, only this time he wasn't wearing his huge cowboy hat. No doubt he had lost his hat as he ambushed me from above.

"Can't talk, huh? Cat got your tongue?" And he slapped me hard across the face. My disjointed jaw swung around like a swing in a storm, nearly hitting the back of my neck. The only thing keeping it in place was the bone and tendons and skin.

Now he gripped me by the throat and lifted. My jaw hung on his hand, bleeding down his arm. "Hmm. I've never seen you before. You must be a newbie. Only a newbie would break in on someone feeding." He pulled me a little closer to his face. My eyes were so blurred I could barely make out the big Texan. "I don't like newbies. Newbies don't get it. Newbies try to change everything. I don't like change."

I couldn't talk, but I could think.

You're killing the little girl.

"Oh, you mean my food source? I suppose so, but food sources know no ages, Newbie, although little girls and boys tend to have a richer, purer blood, which is what I prefer."

You're a fucking animal.

"You don't know me well enough to call me names, little lady. Killing our own kind is looked down upon, but I think I'll make an exception here.

I have a feeling you might make my life difficult if I let you out of here alive."

Now his hand tightened, crushing my throat. I saw his other hand reaching inside his coat pocket. I knew his thoughts. Hell, I was inside his twisted head.

He was reaching for a silver dagger.

I quit flailing and grabbed his hand at my throat with both of my own. I didn't know who the fuck this asshole was, but I knew I wasn't dead yet.

And with all the strength I had, I broke his wrist.

He screamed and dropped me. I landed on my feet and squared off.

"You bitch!"

But I was moving, using all my training and instincts, focusing my fear and hate and anger. I wasn't a slouch. I knew what I was doing. I hit him hard, repeatedly, driving my punches into the face. Who he was, I didn't care. How strong he was, I didn't know. How much damage I was doing, I couldn't tell.

Out of the corner of my eye, I saw Aaron King standing in the doorway, his own jaw hanging down, holding a stun gun. I motioned for him to get the girl, projecting my thoughts to him as strongly as I could. He looked briefly confused and then moved to Maddie.

My brief pause was all Captain Jack needed. He leveled a devastating punch into my right eye. So hard that I heard my cheekbone shatter.

I stumbled backwards and as I did so, I saw something silver slash before me. His dagger. Amazingly, as it came down on me, all I could think of was my kids. I saw their faces. Their beautiful faces. The dagger sliced down, no doubt heading for my heart. Whether or not that would kill me, I didn't know, but I suspected it would. I suspected Captain Jack knew exactly what he was doing.

Except I've been trained in knife fighting. Trained by the best. I did the one thing we were taught to do when there was no real hope of avoiding a plunging knife.

Use my arm as a shield.

And, as I did just that, I heard my old instructor's voice: "Better to cut your arm than to die."

The knife slashed down as my arm came up....

Chapter Fifty-eight

The narrow blade plunged through my arm.

This was shaping up to be a hell of a shitty day. I couldn't even scream. I grunted while my lower jaw flapped.

But, believe it or not, I knew what I was doing. I turned my arm, and the blade came out of his hand. I backed away, stumbling, steam hissing from my forearm where the silver dagger's handle protruded from it.

Gasping and choking on my own blood, I pulled the blade free.

And that's when something snaked across the bedroom, something crackling and alive.

Aaron King's stun gun.

It did little damage to the big Texan in front of me, but the vampire did turn and grab at the wires, and when he did so, I leaped forward, and drove the silver dagger deep into him.

Deep into his heart.

I shrank away as the Texan went into wild convulsions. I had seen death before, but never quite like this. He didn't want to die. That much was clear. His body fought it, clawing at his bloody chest, which hissed steam. He turned to me more than once as if to ask: What the hell have you done? He even lunged at me one more time but didn't get very far.

He collapsed on the tiled floor, back arched, steam rising, holding his chest, gasping like a fish out of water. He did that for an unbelievable amount of time before he finally quit moving.

***

"I've seen some weird shit in my time," said Aaron King next to me. "But this takes the cake."

We were in the living room. Little Maddie was wrapped in blankets and resting in one corner of the voluminous couch. Aaron was sitting next to me, holding my hand, and holding my jaw in place, too.

"You can't talk, I know, but what happened back there..." he started shaking his head, his face paler than any vampire's. "What the hell *did* happen back there?"

I could have reached out with my mind, but I didn't. The old guy seemed to have had enough of a shock. I was just too exhausted to speak, even telepathically.

The bullet had traveled through my stomach

and out my lower back, leaving a hell of a messy hole. Still, the exposure to silver was doing a number on me, leaving me exhausted and nearly unconscious.

"Your poor jaw, lil' darlin'. Your poor arm. Sweet Jesus, what the hell went on back there?" He started shaking his head again, and then I saw there were tears in his eyes. "And what were they doing to this little one? They were taking her blood, weren't they? Is she sick?"

I tried shaking my head. He understood my minute impulse. "No, of course she ain't sick. They're sick. Good Lord, what were they doing to her?"

I tried shaking my head again.

Aaron King said, "Maybe I should quit asking so many questions."

I tried to smile. The old man held my jaw and my arms and did his best to comfort me.

"The paramedics are coming. Tribal police will be here soon, too. We have a hell of a mess on our hands. I don't know where to start explaining or what to say." He looked at me kindly, but I saw the confusion in his eyes. And fear. "You were shot in the stomach, stabbed in the arm. But your wounds have stopped bleeding..."

He let his voice trail off and the old guy just kept holding me and patting me and keeping my poor, broken jaw in place, and we sat like that until the police swarmed into the room....

***

It was late.

I was loaded in the back of an ambulance. It was also coming on morning, which was perhaps an hour or so away. We had spent the night being quizzed from every conceivable angle. Mercifully, Detective Hanner from the Fullerton Police Department had appeared. And once she arrived, things started settling down.

Now Aaron King and I were left alone, and that's when he told me that he had decided to come check things out for himself. He didn't like the idea of me being alone. A few routine questions at the front desk—and no doubt full use of his Southern charm—had led him to connect Carl Luck with the oil-rich Texan. A few more inquiries later and he was on his way up to the suite...when he'd discovered the shattered door.

I nodded and whispered a thank you. Amazingly, I felt my jaw healing. It had also settled back into place; that is, roughly where it should be. Maybe I would forever have an overbite. As Aaron King sat there in the back of the ambulance, holding my hand, Detective Hanner opened the back door. She asked if she could have a moment alone with me, and the old investigator nodded. She told him he was no longer needed and he squeezed my hand lightly and said he would check up on me in a few days.

I nodded and wanted to thank him and I think

he knew how grateful I was to him. Aaron King, who wasn't really Aaron King, nodded to Detective Hanner and left.

Hanner looked at me, then jabbed a thumb in King's direction. "Was that who I think it was?"

I nodded again, and she shook her head and slipped inside the ambulance and shut the door behind her.

"We need to talk," she said.

Chapter Fifty-nine

"Well, I need to talk," she corrected. "I assume your jaw has not healed yet."

I shook my head gingerly.

She leaned over and examined me carefully. "Yeah, that's bad. Give it a day or so and you should be fine. At least, well enough to talk." She lowered her voice further. "Kingsley asked me to talk to you."

She laughed lightly, as I'm sure my eyes just about popped out of my head.

"Yes, I've known Mr. Fulcrum for a long, long time. Probably longer than you've been alive." She sat on the edge of my gurney, resting her hands in her lap, and only occasionally looked me directly in the eyes. And when she did, those few times that our eyes actually met, I had the disconcerting feeling that I was looking at something very alien.

Her eyes were a little too wide. Too searching. Too penetrating. And wild. So damn wild.

She's not human, I thought, and then wondered if she could hear my thoughts, too. Maybe that's why she rarely looked me in the eye. Maybe she knew the effect her eyes had.

Jesus, did I look like that, too?

But Detective Hanner did not give me any indication that she had heard my thoughts. Or maybe I was getting better at shielding them. I didn't know. There was still so much to learn.

"Kingsley told me that you might have the medallion. He was sketchy on this, as he knows its importance and value. And he is right in not being too forthcoming about this. People will kill for that medallion. Vampires especially. You see, not all of us desire our current state. Some of us wish to be human again."

Her eyes flashed over mine briefly, and her pupils were nothing more than tiny black pinpricks. Her eyes continued over my face and settled on my jaw.

"He thought he could trust me, and that I might help you."

She looked at me again, and I suddenly realized how vulnerable I was in this position. Her pupils flared briefly, and she nodded. "He's right, of course. You can trust me." She looked at my arm, cocking her head to one side. "But you shouldn't take my word for it. There's many like us who aren't honorable. There are many like us who are like him—" and here she nodded to another ambulance where I knew lay two bodies, Carl Luck and Captain Jack— "Yes, there are many who rape and pillage and act like asses. Just like humans, I suppose.

"But you can trust me, even if you don't yet." She rested her hand lightly on my leg and hers was an oddly comforting touch. I say oddly because I could feel the cold radiating through the blanket. "Long ago, I had a child once, too. He died of old age, and I watched him die from a distance, never getting close enough for him to recognize me. He, of course, thought his mother had died in a fire, as I had planned. You see, he was getting too old, and his mother was staying so young. It was the hardest decision I ever had to make." She smiled weakly at me. "But I watched him from afar, helping him when he needed it. I suspect he thought he had a guardian angel. But little did he know it was just me." She smiled again. "Lord help anyone who crossed him."

She laughed lightly and so did I. Mostly, though, I was entranced by her. Enchanted, even. *She's like me,* I kept thinking. *She's like me. And I'm not alone.*

"We do not have much time, Samantha. I will take care of things on this end. Some killings are not as heavily investigated as others. Some people need to be convinced of this. I suspect, by the time everyone leaves here tonight, they will be convinced that this had been a drug deal gone bad.

Very, very bad.

"Oh, and the body of Captain Jack? Not to worry. He will decompose like anyone else. As far as the authorities are concerned, he is just another dead man. And not the creature he had been."

She looked at me again, and her alien eyes briefly locked onto mine. "I have already convinced them to let you go. In fact, many of the police here have no idea why you are here." She smiled slyly. "Yes, I have been a vampire for a long, long time. I know things. You and I need to talk."

I nodded. Yes, we very much needed to talk.

And now she reached out and took my hand and the cold that permeated from her was shocking. I did my best not to gasp. "But first, you must take care of your little one. Do what you need to do, Samantha Moon, and I will help you find the answers you seek. Answers about the medallion..." Her voice trailed off. "But know this: There are no guarantees. Few know anything about this medallion. And those who do may not talk. Those who do, may, in fact, be dead."

I nodded and felt the tears come to me. So many tears these past few days. Detective Hanner squeezed my hand a little tighter. Two ice cold hands.

"I don't envy you, Samantha. I don't know you, of course. But I don't envy you. You have a decision to make. Perhaps the most difficult decision I can imagine."

Detective Hanner released my hand and came

over to my side and hugged me deeply, careful of my jaw. As she held me, I wept into her shoulder.

Chapter Sixty

I was flying over the Pacific Ocean.

It was the next night. I had spent the day by my son's side, holding his hands, even as the doctors had raced in and out of the hospital. Some screamed at me to get out of the way. One even shoved me out of the way. They fought for his life. They fought hard to save him.

I watched from his bedside as the doctors used all their skill and medicines and machines. One doctor told me to expect the worst. To start making preparations. I told him to go to hell.

My son, for now, was still hanging on. Still alive.

For now.

The ocean was black and infinite. Crazy, glowing lights zigzagged beneath the surface, some bigger than others, and I knew this was life. Ocean life. Some of the bigger shapes didn't zig or zag so much as lumber slowly through the ocean, sometimes surfacing and blowing out great sprays of water that refracted the moonlight.

I flapped my massive wings languidly, riding the tides of night. Cold wind blew over my perfectly aerodynamic body.

It had been a hell of a day. The black halo around my son was so dense. Nearly syrupy. He had only hours to live, I knew it. Danny was by his side. And so was my sister and my daughter. Sherbet had stopped by, and so had Fang and Kingsley. Mercifully at separate times. Aaron King, Knighthorse and Spinoza all stopped by, too, each bringing flowers. Aaron King checked my jaw, saw me talking, and just shook his head in wonder. Knighthorse and Spinoza were both irked that they had not been invited to the big showdown at the casino, until I reminded them I was a highly trained federal agent who could take care of herself.

The air was cold. Perhaps even freezing, but I felt perfectly comfortable. The moon was only half full overhead.

Had it really been only two weeks ago that the hulking monster that was Kingsley had appeared in my hotel suite?

I had checked on Maddie, too. The little girl was going to make it. She had needed a full blood transfusion. The black halo around her little body had all but disappeared.

The specialist from Chicago had arrived, too,

along with another colleague of his. The agreement was unilateral: my son had a particularly aggressive form of Kawasaki Disease. Already three doses of intravenous immunoglobulin had been administered to Anthony. Most children respond within 24 hours to the first dose. My son showed no signs of responding. They next tried salicylate therapy and corticosteroids. Neither worked. Finally, they tried cyclophosphamide and plasma exchange, experimental treatments with variable outcomes. Nothing worked.

I had listened to the doctors conferring with each other from across the room. They didn't know that I could hear them, of course. One doctor mentioned that there was nothing left to try. The other doctor nodded grimly. The first doctor came over to me and gave me the bad news. My son was not responding to any treatments, he said. I asked what that meant, and he looked at me sadly, and said sometimes children pull through. He didn't sound very hopeful.

Sometimes they pull through, he said, but I heard him think: *and sometimes they die, too.*

The wind seemed to pick up from behind me, and I soared effortlessly. Below me, the pod of whales seemed to be keeping pace, their glowing bodies surfacing and spraying. I quickly swept past them.

I thought of the water. The dark water. The world seemed to slow down under water. Sound became muted, and light diffused.

I looked down again...stopped flapping, then tucked my wings in and dove.

***

I closed my eyes as I broke the surface.

My aerodynamic body cut easily through the water, and I shot down into the dark depths. But the water, much like the air, wasn't truly dark. Sparks of light zipped through it. Bright filaments that lit my way.

I flapped my wings and discovered to my great surprise and pleasure that I easily moved through the water, my wings expelling it behind me powerfully, moving me quickly along. Like a manta ray. I was a giant, bat-shaped manta ray.

I flapped my wings slowly but powerfully. Water surged past me, but did not hurt my eyes. This creature that I had become was amazingly adaptive and resilient.

I was amazingly adaptive and resilient.

But not my son. No, my son was dying, and he would be dead within hours. I knew it. The doctors knew it. Everyone knew it. You did not need to be a doctor or a psychic to see the encroachment of death.

I could stop his death. I could give him eternal life, in fact. I could have my baby boy by my side forever. Detective Hanner had told me how to do it. The process of transformation. Of turning mortal into immortal.

It was a crazy idea. A reckless idea.

But I could save him—and then later return his mortality to him with the medallion.

Maybe. Except no one seemed to know for sure.

I continued flapping, my heart heavy. A creature sidled up next to me. A dolphin. No, two dolphins. They kept pace with me, thrusting with their powerful tails. I knew very little about dolphins but if I had to guess, they looked perplexed as hell. I didn't blame them. No doubt they had never seen the likes of me. A moment later, they peeled away, their auras leaving behind brightly phosphorescent vapor trails.

My son was going to die within hours. Maybe sooner.

This much was true.

I could save him. Giving him eternal life.

And I possessed a legendary medallion that could give him back his mortality. A loophole in death.

Not too many people had that option.

Not too many mothers. Desperate mothers.

I heard Kingsley's words again. *And what if you can't change him back, Sam?*

Anthony would be immortal. At age seven. Doomed to walk the earth forever. At age seven. To drink blood for all eternity.

At age seven.

It was one thing to consider turning the handsome, love-struck Fang into my immortal lover, someone who wanted to fill my nights with pleasure and companionship, perhaps for the rest of my existence, which could be thousands of years, but who knew? It was quite another thing to doom Anthony, my precious, precious child, to that same fate—he would always be seven years old, and a vampire. I could not even imagine how to explain it all to him if the medallion did not work.

My heart gave a tremendous heave.

I didn't know what to do. Who could possibly know what to do?

Time was running out.

My son was dying.

I tipped one of my wings and veered back toward the direction I had come.

My mind raced as I flapped hard, surging through the water, scattering tiny silver fish before me.

And then I came to a decision.

God, help me, I came to a decision.

I flapped my wings as hard as I could and burst free from the ocean and shot up into the night sky.

The End

About the Author:

J.R. Rain is an ex-private investigator who now writes full-time. He lives in a small house on a small island with his small dog, Sadie. Please visit him at www.jrrain.com.

Made in the USA
Monee, IL
25 June 2023